THE BROKEN BARGAIN

Dominic placed his hands on either side of Nerissa's face and drew it toward him. His mouth, she discovered, tasted of spices and wine, intoxicating than

"I've never done said.

"Done what?" she ...lessly.

"Seduced a lady. For that, you know," he said, "is exactly what I'm doing. To speak more plainly, will you lie with me tonight, sweet Nerissa?"

"I'm not your wife," she said, and took a backward step. "That isn't part of our arrangement."

"True," he agreed. "But you might be interested in renegotiating the terms."

MARGARET EVANS PORTER's love of the Irish countryside shows on every page of her writing. She is a native of Georgia, educated in England, and currently divides her time between Denver and New England.

ROAD
TO RUIN

by

Margaret Evans Porter

A SIGNET BOOK

SIGNET
Published by the Penguin Group
Penguin Books USA Inc., 375 Hudson Street,
New York, New York 10014, U.S.A.
Penguin Books Ltd, 27 Wrights Lane,
London W8 5TZ, England
Penguin Books Australia Ltd, Ringwood,
Victoria, Australia
Penguin Books Canada Ltd, 10 Alcorn Avenue,
Toronto, Ontario, Canada M4V 3B2
Penguin Books (N.Z.) Ltd, 182–190 Wairau Road,
Auckland 10, New Zealand

Penguin Books Ltd, Registered Offices:
Harmondsworth, Middlesex, England

Published by Signet, an imprint of New American Library, a division of
Penguin Books USA Inc. Published by arrangement with Walker and Company.

First Signet Printing, December, 1992
10 9 8 7 6 5 4 3 2 1

Now go we in content
To liberty and not to banishment

—Shakespeare,
AS YOU LIKE IT, I, iii

Prologue

THE SCRATCH OF a quill pen upon paper was amplified by the quiet of the wood-panelled library, where a lady sat at a writing desk, her dark head bent as she wrote. The sombre grey of her gown, which suggested a recent bereavement, did not conceal her charms. She was strikingly lovely, with a pair of indigo eyes accentuated by bold, arching brows. Nature had cleverly placed a beauty mark near her generously shaped mouth, drawing attention to its pleasing shape.

The room was still, lit only by the fading afternoon sun, and golden motes of dust danced in the rays that slanted in through the windows. The chairs were shrouded in hollandcloth, and the table tops were bare of any ornament. Several paintings leaned sadly against the wainscoting, and although the grate gleamed from a recent and thorough blacking, there was no fire in it. Even the long-case clock was silent, for it had not been wound this day.

That Nerissa Newby had been busy at her task for some time was evident from the small pile of folded notes that had accumulated at her elbow. Suddenly her swiftly moving hand stilled, and while she searched her mind for a word or phrase, she stared out of the nearest window, left open to admit the fresh air. October was not yet a week old; the weather was pleasantly dry and mild, and with the leaves of the trees on the turn, the landscape was a pleasing mix of green and golden tints. In the distance, Nerissa could see the tall, narrow spire of the local church, which pointed skyward as if to pierce the bright blue heavens.

In its time, the Buckinghamshire village had withstood flame, flood, and enclosures. It had also been immortalised in the verses of the poet Cowper. But Nerissa, who much preferred the architectural varieties of London, had never been fond of Olney. The high street, though broad, was lined with stone buildings that had always seemed to her to be as stern and unlovely as their inhabitants. Nearly all the roofs were tiled now, but the cottages that sheltered the less affluent were still covered with thatch, which had contributed to the spread of a great fire many years ago. The flames had ravaged the town, consuming forty-eight dwellings, as well as numerous barns and outbuildings. Nerissa had been a child at the time, and she would never forget the alarming spectacle of gutted houses, and the pall of acrid smoke that had lain over the neighbourhood for days after.

She transferred her gaze from the church steeple to a small cottage just visible through the trees. No plume of smoke wafted from the chimney today, and its absence was a painful reminder of yet another loss. Catching her lower lip between her teeth, she resumed her writing. But her industry was short-lived, for she heard the sound of hoofbeats in the lane, and put down her quill again. The rider, a fair-haired gentleman, was approaching her house, but she sat perfectly still until she heard the heavy, ominous pounding of the door-knocker. Then she rose, almost reluctantly, with a slow, languorous grace, and made her way to the dark hallway, carefully stepping around a pair of corded trunks.

When she opened the front door to her visitor, his handsome face revealed his surprise. "But where is Mary?" he asked.

"She is much occupied just now," Nerissa replied. "Do come in, Andrew."

He entered, his eyes widening when she led him past the trunks into the hall. The state of the library affected him powerfully, and he looked about in consternation. "Nerissa, what is going on here?"

Before answering she smoothed a tendril of mahogany hair which had escaped the coil atop her head. In a firm, clear voice she replied, "I am closing up my house, Andrew. I summoned you here to tell you so. And also to ask what the *devil* you've done with Lucy Roberts—and the child."

"I thought I forbade you to go to that cottage again," Andrew said severely.

During the twenty-three years of her life, Nerissa Newby had heeded one person only, and he was six months dead. "I am not some child to be ordered about, nor have I yet taken any vow to obey you," she said pithily. "As for my visit to Lucy, I had a purpose in going—I owed her a quarter's wages at Michaelmas."

"She was paid." He avoided the smouldering blue eyes she had turned upon him.

"You sent them away, didn't you?"

Andrew Hudgins drew himself up to his full height. "Nerissa, I could hardly stand by and let the common folk gossip about my future wife. And I have four unmarried sisters to think of. Not only you, but my whole family have suffered from your association with that low woman and her ill-gotten brat."

"Don't call her that!" Nerissa struggled to control her rising temper, and succeeded well enough to say in a less volatile manner, "He is called Samuel. I named him myself."

"That may be, but it's hardly a boasting matter."

"Neither is bustling the pair of them off in that furtive way—it only confirms the rumours flying thick and fast from Olney to Weston Underwood to Clifton Reynes.''

"I did what had to be done, and I refuse to justify my action beyond that. The girl has gone to live with her mother, and there's an end to it.''

His stubborn certainty that he had acted correctly vexed Nerissa beyond the limits of her endurance. "But you've done the worst possible thing, don't you see?'' she cried. "You might just as well have printed a placard with the most damning version of the story and hung it in the marketplace for all to read.'' Lifting her chin, she continued in a declamatory voice. " 'Miss Newby, while living with her father in London, gave birth to a love-child. The captain, an unconventional fellow, let her keep it, and together they passed it off as the washer-woman's brat.' ''

Andrew said repressively, "I find this conversation in very poor taste, Nerissa.''

"Well, you brought it upon yourself,'' she told him bluntly.

"The possibility that you are the mother of that infant is quite absurd,'' he said. "There may be some slight resemblance, enough to arouse comment, but you need not fear that I would ever condemn you on such flimsy evidence.''

"And what of your mother?'' she retorted. "No fortune, not even mine, is great enough to induce her to swallow scandal-broth so hot and rich and spicy!'' Nerissa took an agitated turn about the room, her skirts rustling with each energetic step. Suddenly coming to a halt, she said wearily, "What's done is done. With Lucy and Samuel gone, at least I can console myself with the fact that they are well out of this coil. And *I* mean to be as soon as I possibly can, otherwise the talk will never die down.''

"When may I expect you to return?''

"I don't know that I will ever return.'' Seeing how

disturbed he was by her candid and unequivocal reply,
Nerissa said more gently, "I'm sorry to pain you, Andrew, truly, but I think upon reflexion you will agree
that it is for the best. As fond of you as I have always
been, I am not—I will never be the wife you deserve."

She walked over to the desk and picked up the fine
sapphire ring which had formerly graced her left hand.
When she held it out to him, her face wore a faint,
self-mocking smile. "You stand too much upon good
form to ever cry off, especially now I'm in a scrape.
My reputation is already so tarnished that being called
a jilt will hardly make a difference. Or perhaps they
will say you jilted me—for I well know I've given you
a good enough cause to do so."

He drew a deep breath, expelling it in a long, re-
gretful sigh, but he did take the ring from her. "Will
you go to your cousins in London?" he asked quietly.

She was thankful for his calm, unemotional acceptance of the blow she had dealt him. But that was to
be expected; he was a gentleman and as such would
make it easy for her, whatever he felt inside. Maybe
he had known, deep down, that this rift was inevitable,
and had prepared himself for it. "Never London," she
said, shaking her head. "I couldn't face all the necessary explanations, not just now." Her shoulders
sagged, but she squared them almost at once. "And
without Papa, I think I would have a hard time of it,
living in town. No, I have decided to pay a long visit
to my friend Mrs. Sedgewick, who lives in Staffordshire. I leave tomorrow."

There was very little more to be said. Nerissa gave
him her letters, asking if he would be so kind as to
post them for her. One was to her trustees in London,
informing them of the termination of her engagement.
Another was for Andrew's mother and sisters, thanking them for their many kindnesses to her after her
father's death. Although neither their attentions nor her

gratitude had been completely heartfelt, Nerissa knew her duty to his family.

"I am writing a reference for Mary," she continued. "And if you should hear of anyone in need of a groom, perhaps you could recommend Alfred. One of the maidservants has already found a new place, and the other will go to Northampton to work for a wool-comber. And speaking of Northampton, I have decided to hire a post-chaise there, to avoid notice."

"I shall convey you there at whatever hour you please."

Politely but firmly she refused this offer. "John has already offered to drive me in the gig."

"You have discussed this with my brother?"

She nodded, and saw that this distressed him as much as the return of the sapphire ring. "I couldn't tell you of my plan to leave," she explained, "because I didn't want to worry you any more than I've done already. For pride's sake I'm determined to be far away before it becomes generally known. And before you begin to regret ever knowing me."

Staring down at the ring he held, Andrew said, "I don't believe I do know you, Nerissa. Not really, not as I've always wished I might. It's to be farewell, then?"

"It must be," she replied, striving to keep her voice steady, for this part was far more difficult than she had anticipated. He was a good man, he had always been her friend, but he would never be her husband. To hold out false hope would be too cruel, and her father had always taught her to be fair in all her dealings.

His attempt to smile was not entirely successful. "After all this time, I don't quite know how to say good-bye—until a few moments ago, I believed we would be spending the rest of our lives together. It is what I always dreamed of, you know, even when you were a wild little girl—the delight of your papa and

the despair of your aunt. Good-bye, Nerissa.'' He
kissed her cheek in the same tentative, brotherly way
she had grown used to, and left her standing in the
middle of the darkening room, surrounded by the
ghostly, cloth-covered chairs.

She crossed to the window to watch her erstwhile
fiance ride off towards the village. A chapter in her
life was forever closed—several chapters, in fact, and
she ought to be glad of it, for none of the more recent
ones had been very pleasant. It was not her way to
repine, yet she couldn't help wishing for her father's
comforting presence, though she knew what he would
tell her, in his bracing, salt-laced language. Determined not to give way to despair, she whispered the
oft-spoken creed: ''A calm sea makes for a dull voy-
age.''

But oh, how smooth and easy her passage through
life would have been if she had been born dull and
plain, like Andrew's older sisters, Ruth and Judith, for
then her good name would never have been sullied by
suspicion. And even if she had possessed the common
prettiness and flirtatious ways of Sarah and Rebecca
Hudgins, not a soul would have whispered that she had
borne a bastard child. But Nerissa Newby's face was
neither plain nor pretty, but something else altogether,
and it had damned her.

1

HIGH ABOVE THE vast, busy city, the black velvet canopy of sky was adorned with numberless, diamond-like stars. The evening was several hours old, but the fashionable part of London had only just come alive. Faint strains of music and bursts of muted laughter from Mayfair's most notable residences drifted into the night, mingling with the cry of the watchman and the clatter of hooves on pavement.

Clifford Street, to the east of Berkeley Square, was less busy on this October night when so many of London's elite were abroad. Although Number Seven had received its share of visitors when it was the principal residence of a political giant, now it was shuttered and silent. Lord Sidmouth, formerly His Majesty's chief minister, was no longer in power; Mr. Pitt, his abler predecessor, had retained the royal favour. Because his lordship lived retired at White Lodge at Richmond, a gift to him from a grateful sovereign, he seldom visited Number Seven. Clifford Street was poorer for his neglect.

Most of the residences lining the street were quiet, but several doors down from Sidmouth's celebrated address an evening party was in progress, to the delight of the children living in the house across the way. Three boys had gathered at an upper window to observe the comings and goings, but because these occurred at uncertain intervals, they were growing bored and were on the point of giving up the vigil. Their interest revived when a town carriage came into view, drawn by four horses, their satiny coats gleaming in the diffuse light of the street lamps. The proud bearing of the liveried coachman on the box and the swift efficiency of the bewigged footman who climbed down from his perch to open the door were similarly impressive. The possessor of this handsome turn-out, whoever he might be, was no commoner: a family crest was visible on the door of the coach. The children waited breathlessly for the bearer of these arms to emerge.

When a tall, cloaked figure climbed out of the carriage and turned to address his footman, the boys leaned even more precariously over the sill. There was no mistaking the servant's reply, a respectful, "Yes, milord."

The resulting babble of excited voices overhead reached the ears of this lordly gentleman, who immediately glanced up. Seeing that row of nightshirted urchins framed by the window, Dominic Sebastian Charles Blythe, second Baron Blythe, was forcibly reminded of the long-ago nights when he had stood at his bedroom window to observe the evening traffic in Grosvenor Square. Prompted by this sharp stab of nostalgia, and with a beautiful disregard for the butler who had opened the front door to him, he raised his arm in salutation.

His youthful admirers, overwhelmed by this splendid act of condescension, gleefully returned the compliment.

His lordship, now fully caught in the game, waved back. To his sorrow, a shadowy figure—unmistakably female—bustled the lads out of sight and followed this act of cruelty by slamming the window shut. Dominic turned towards the house, and when he entered it he grinned shamelessly at his host's butler, a witness to

his indiscretion. Removing his long cape, he handed
it to the footman who stood at the bottom of the
staircase. At the top stood the couple whose recent
marriage was being celebrated this night.

Although his felicitations would be genuine, a certain irony attended them. Dominic had known Sir
Algernon Titus all his life, but he was more intimately
acquainted with the baronet's bride, with whom he'd
spent a riotous fortnight at Brighton some six years
ago. The workings of fate were curious indeed: his
own former mistress—if that term was applicable,
given the brevity of their association—was now the
wedded wife of one of his closest friends.

The lady herself was not unaware of the irony. Lady
Titus, watching as the baron ascended the staircase,
smiled upon him in a way that would have given her
elderly husband pause, had his attention not also been
on the newcomer. In evening attire, Lord Blythe was
a study in stark contrasts, for he wore a black coat
over a snowy shirt, black satin knee breeches, white
silk hose that fitted and flattered his long legs, and a
pair of glossy black pumps. His colouring, too, was
all black and white, the thick, straight hair was as dark
as midnight, his fine-boned face as pale and luminous
as the moon. But even if he had been as ugly as a
gargoyle, Lady Titus would have received him thankfully. For the past hour, too few had entered her house,
far too many had left it, and she was desperate for the
sight of a new face.

She had been born Miss Georgiana Symonds, and
in her seventeenth year had eloped with a dashing
young lieutenant. Three years later, the war with
France made her a widow, but already her reputation
was such that none of the numerous gentlemen so eager to console her offered anything more than *carte
blanche*—which she had occasionally accepted. After
a campaign of two years, she had finally lured a bar-

onet to the altar, no mean achievement for a humbly born lady of twenty-seven years. But this, her first evening party since becoming Lady Titus, had attracted very few of the fashionable persons to whom she had wished to display her matrimonial triumph, and her new husband's curling lip and satirical eye were provoking in the extreme. She had given dozens of parties during her first marriage, and even more during her dashing widowhood, and all had been successful. To be sure, some had also been attended by a measure of notoriety, but it wasn't kind of Algy to remind her of that, not now that she was respectably married again. She glanced at the greying head of the gentleman standing at her side, thinking pettishly that the worst thing about older men, apart form their inordinate jealousy and an outsized sensitivity about their age, was that air of insufferable superiority.

When the handsome nobleman bowed over her hand, Georgiana sucked in her breath, thereby increasing the swell of bosom that was barely concealed by her low décolletage. "Why, Blythe, how good of you to come," she murmured, surreptitiously squeezing his fingers. But despite the warmth of this welcome, she received only an impersonal nod before Lord Blythe moved on to shake hands with her husband.

"Dominic, my dear boy," Sir Algernon Titus greeted the newcomer. "I warned Georgie not to count on seeing you tonight, but I must say I've never been happier to be proved wrong. Finally returned to town, eh?"

"As you see, sir," Lord Blythe replied. His voice was low, with a slight huskiness that enhanced rather than detracted from its appeal. "Some trifling business with the settlement of my father's estate brought me back to town sooner than I wished. But not soon enough—I would have liked to offer my toast at your nuptials." His grey eyes flickered towards the opulent blonde, whose satin gown matched the warm, creamy tones of her overexposed flesh.

The baronet shrugged. "It was a simple affair. I persuaded Georgie that the spectacle of a man my age taking a wife was absurd enough without the attendant pomp and ceremony."

"What Algy means is," the bride announced unblushingly and with a saucy toss of her head, "he was afraid of gossip. But it's not as though he's the first man to marry his mistress."

"Nor will I be the last," her husband declared before turning his attention back to their guest. "The young Marquis of Elston is here, with some cousin of yours in tow. Says he's Cavender's brother."

"What? Not Justin?" Dominic asked in surprise. "I must ask him how Lincoln's Inn suits him after the rigours of Oxford."

Sir Algernon chuckled. "Oh, aye, these young men do wear their brains out at university, don't they? I tell you, Dominic, I see something of your father in the boy, and don't doubt that he'll be lording it over some ministry office before many years have passed. I hope I live to see it. But what title will our king find for him, I wonder? Your father was rewarded with a barony, but Justin might go higher yet. And with his brother a viscount in his own right, I predict you Blythes will hold a monopoly on titles someday."

His lordship laughed. "It may well come to pass, sir, but Justin has a long way to go yet. My father's honours came late in life, and after many years of service to the Crown."

After he and his host exchanged a few remarks of a less personal nature, Dominic went to the saloon, so sparsely populated that he sighted his quarry with no difficulty. Two well-favoured young men in their early twenties stood side by side, the brown head of one bent close to the bright gold one of the other. He approached this pair from behind, clapped his cousin on the shoulder, and intoned, "Justin Richard Blythe, for the crime of dereliction of duty I arrest you in the name of the law."

The young man so named whirled around, clearly shocked, but when he saw who had accosted him, he cried out in delight. "Nick! What the devil are you doing here?"

"I might ask the same of you, stripling. Have you deserted your law studies so soon after beginning them?"

"You're taking the wrong man to task. The blame rests entirely with this fellow," said the Honourable Justin Blythe, indicating his companion. His leaf-brown eyes twinkled with mischief as he explained, "Cousin Damon forced me to accompany him, you see, and I am here very much against my will."

Damon Lovell, Marquis of Elston, exhibited a lazy smile. "My dear Nick, do not begrudge Justin this night on the town. We poor mortals must cram what pleasures we can into our brief time on this earth."

Dominic shook his head. "Clearly you are bent on corrupting my cousin."

"*My* cousin, too," the marquis reminded him. "Through our mothers."

"And yet," Justin interposed, "despite our tie of blood, I never met Cousin Damon till our paths crossed at Oxford. What an odd family we are!"

Said Dominic, with mock gravity, "You acknowledge the connexion? But I warn you, this cousin of yours is quite notorious—the most shocking example of hedonism to be found among all the noble houses of this land." The two younger men laughed, and he continued. "What brings you to Sir Algernon's house tonight, Damon?"

"Curiosity," drawled the marquis.

Dominic lifted his black brows quizzically. "Oh?

but the lovely Georgiana's reputation is really no worse than that of any other society lady, however common her origins." He swiftly inspected the assembled company, and added, "When she sent out her cards, she certainly gave the preference to peahens and peacocks." He added, "Have you noticed how all the ladies are so shrill and charmless and unlovely, and their mates so very ornamental?"

The truth of the latter part of his observation was borne out by the three gentlemen themselves. Both the baron and the marquis were dressed in the height of the mode, with an elegance that surpassed the efforts of other men. But in every other respect, they were perfect foils: Lord Blythe's black hair found its opposite in Lord Elston's gilt locks. And his lean, aristocratic face resembled polished marble, while his friend's features looked as if they had been sculpted from alabaster. Although Justin Blythe presented a less dramatic appearance than either of their lordships, he was memorable in his own right with his chestnut crop, merry eyes, and air of quiet assurance. They made a most attractive grouping.

The ladies present, however, would have preferred to divide that arresting trio and draw lots for the individual components. Each of the two noblemen had his own set of devotées, ranged on opposite sides of the question of whether the baron or the marquis was the more worthy of admiration. Now that another promising member of the family had arrived on the social scene in the pleasing person of Justin, a third faction was forming. Many a member of the fair sex, wearied of a husband or bored with her paramour, would happily overlook his status as a younger son, since position and wealth, so indispensable in a mate, were negligible qualities in a lover.

But it was war, not love which occupied the three gentlemen, who were discussing Lord Nelson's ineffectual pursuit of Villeneuve and the French fleet. Said the marquis, shaking his bright head, "He chased the Frogs all the way to the West Indies, and to no avail. The great confrontation we've hoped for is still before us, rather than a settled thing."

"The Lords of Admiralty appear to be satisfied with Nelson's abilities," Dominic commented. "He only sailed from Portsmouth a mere three weeks ago, so we need not despair about his present campaign quite yet."

His friend's reply was drowned out by a sudden cry from Justin. "Look there, it's my brother—see, he's standing by the door."

"So he is," Dominic observed. "Cousin Ramsey's presence at this gathering is even more of a surprise than yours, Damon."

Lord Elston concurred, saying grimly, "One would expect to find Ram in the shires at this season. Can it be that he lacks the funds to keep up his hunting?"

"I would advise against raising that question," Dominic warned him.

The Twelfth Viscount Cavender was a thickset, stocky gentleman, whose athletic build, tanned complexion and gold-streaked brown hair attested to many hours spent in the saddle. He was greeted warmly by Justin, with less enthusiasm by his fellow peers, and he, in turn, was no more than coolly civil to them.

"So, Nick, you've returned from Wiltshire," he remarked. "Surely you haven't wearied of playing farmer?"

"Never that," Dominic replied imperturbably. "Blythe was looking its best, and I hated to tear myself away. By the by, while I was in the neighbourhood I took it upon myself to look in at Cavender Chase. Your tenant appears to be well satisfied, and so should you be with his management."

Viscount Cavender's sun-bronzed face clouded over

at the mention of his ancestral home, and he said stiffly, "You needn't have troubled yourself. My agent sends regular reports, you know."

"I do know, but your agent isn't a member of the family," Dominic pointed out. "That reminds me," he said, turning to the marquis, "I chanced to meet your bailiff on the Bath Road one day, Damon. Without saying it directly, he left me with the impression that you've neglected to visit Elston Towers since you came of age—three years now, isn't it?"

Lord Elston's blue eyes were suddenly as hard and cold as ice, but his voice was as languid as ever when he replied, "True, but so long as the estate continues to return a profit, I care nothing for it. The place has never been a home to me."

Justin Blythe, conscious of the tension around him, tried to ease it with a laugh and a jest. "Admit it, Damon, you're a Sussex man at heart and by habit. Even so, you were born in Wiltshire and your lands march with ours, and thus we have a greater claim upon your loyalties."

The sudden burst of masculine laughter reached the ears of Lady Titus, who had given up her post on the staircase to glide in and out among her guests. When she reached the quartet in the corner, she favoured Mr. Blythe with a smile and expressed the hope that he had enjoyed himself since his arrival in London.

Justin, politely averting his eyes from her low neckline, assured her that he had. "Cousin Damon persists in telling me how tiresome the city is at this time of year, and even Dominic agrees. But if this is their notion of dullness, they must be sadly spoiled."

Georgiana beamed her pleasure at what she deemed a compliment to her party, and she added in a confidential tone, "My dear sir, I believe they are." Transferring her melting gaze to Dominic, she murmured, "Lord Blythe, you must be tutoring your young cousin

in gallantry. I vow, he could not wish for a more prac-
ticed instructor in the art of pleasing the ladies.''

Her words sparked a flash of fury in Viscount Cavender's brown eyes. It was fleeting, but Georgiana saw
it. She knew she'd made a mistake by raising his ire,
however inadvertently, for he was a vengeful man.
Thinking it best to efface herself, she said, ''I really
must go warn my butler that we won't be needing *quite*
all of the champagne we ordered for tonight. Pray excuse me, gentlemen.''

Her silent prayer that Lord Cavender would not take
her to task went unanswered. A little while later he
accosted her, and his expression caused her to say nervously, ''Enact no scenes here, my lord. Remember
whose house this is—whose guest you are.''

''You failed me last night,'' he growled.

''I couldn't help it. Algy didn't go to his club after
all.''

''You're lying, Georgie. I saw him there with my
own eyes, and when he settled down to a game of
whist, I dashed back to my lodgings. Where were
you?''

She shrugged one bare shoulder, and the gesture was
eloquent of nonchalance. ''I can't arrange our meetings so easily as I did before my marriage,'' she told
him. ''How many times must I remind you? It's imperative that we be discreet.''

''Discreet?'' he repeated under his breath. ''And I
suppose that's what you were being just now, when
you were flirting with Blythe!''

Georgiana reflected, not for the first time, that her
lover was much less attractive in anger than when he
was in one of his rare good moods. To appease him,
she trilled a disclaimer. ''Flirting with Lord Blythe?
What an absurd accusation!''

''Is it? You fancied him once, and it's my suspicion

you mean to have him back again—now that you've secured your baronet.'' He ground his teeth savagely.

''He already has a mistress, as you know very well. Oh, *how* you bore me with your passions and jealous pets,'' she cried, momentarily forgetting how her disdain might be received by this volatile gentleman. ''My *affaire* with Nick Blythe is ancient history, so brief and so long ago that even Algy, who knows the worst about me, never heard of it. Honestly, Ram, your rivalry with your cousin is too tedious for words. Sometimes I think it's the only reason you sought me out in the first place.''

''Come to me tomorrow night,'' he replied, ''and give me the chance to prove otherwise.''

She shook her head, and the golden ringlets bobbed.

''Damn you, Georgie—''

''I promise I'll contrive another meeting soon, but only if you leave now. Algy is no fool, and more observant than you may think. He's also quite a good shot, and we wouldn't want to put him in the position of defending my honour, however tattered it may be.''

Ramsey made no move to go. ''Meet me tomorrow, in Carrington Street.'' But Georgiana only smiled wearily and walked away from him without giving him the answer he'd demanded of her. He glared after her retreating figure, oblivious to his watchful host's approach.

When he heard Sir Algernon say reflectively, ''Poor Georgie, she is all aflutter tonight,'' he turned around to find the baronet standing near.

Uncertain of how much, if anything, Georgiana's husband had overheard, Ramsey said diffidently, ''So I perceive. Why should that be, I wonder?''

''Oh, several possibilities leap to mind. She is preoccupied with her duties as hostess, perhaps, or too conscious of being on view at her first public appearance as Lady Titus.''

Ramsey regarded the baronet through hostile eyes. "Or could she, perchance, be discomfitted by the presence of someone from her past?"

Sir Algernon smiled, but in a decidedly unpleasant fashion. "To the best of my knowledge, I am the only gentleman who matches that description."

"You are much mistaken in that assumption, sir," Ramsey told him harshly.

The older man maintained his composure, although the strain of it showed in his face. "I listen to no tales about my wife. And by God, Cavender, you'll keep your distance from her—or answer for it!"

"Fling your threats at my cousin Dominic's head, not mine," the viscount retorted.

"What the devil are you implying?" the baronet thundered.

"Merely that you would do better to investigate the questionable nature of Lord Blythe's relations with Lady Titus—past *and* present!" On that wrathful note, Ramsey stalked off.

A few hours later, when the birds were first beginning to stir, a solemn cavalcade of two riders and a horse-drawn carriage arrived at Chalk Farm. The sun had not yet shown its face; its advent was heralded by a pink haze in the eastern sky, which threw Primrose Hill into the dark, ominous silhouette. Lord Elston, Mr. Justin Blythe, and a pale young man who clutched a small black bag climbed out of the coach. These three conversed in controlled, clipped voices, but the two horsemen, who had dismounted, said nothing.

Bred though Dominic Blythe had been to revere and uphold the honourable code, he now found himself questioning its validity for the first time. He was about to exchange pistol shots with a man old enough to be his father, who had, in fact, been his own father's good friend. And a good friend to him as well, until last night.

When Sir Algernon, his face red with fury, had cornered him and flung an insupportable insult to his head, he'd believed his host had partaken too freely of champagne. It would have been within his rights to demand satisfaction, but instead he had apologised for whatever fault he had committed, all unwitting. The older gentleman, even more incensed, had called him a lying blackguard and had insisted that they meet at dawn to settle their differences. Dominic, knowing that a refusal would cast doubt upon his honour, which Sir Algernon had called into question, could do nothing else but accept the challenge. Whereupon he had left the soirée, never fearing that Justin and Damon would somehow mediate the bizarre, unprovoked quarrel. He returned to his house in Grosvenor Square, expecting that he would soon receive a letter of apology from the baronet, but the only note delivered into his hand came from Damon's pen, specifying the time and place of the meeting. Experienced in these matters, Dominic had resigned himself to the inevitable. He knew the chance for a reconciliation between two parties was directly proportionate to the length of time that elapsed between the challenge and the duel itself. This one would not be averted.

Now, as the morning breeze whipped at his hair, he cursed himself for attending that party. And he wished he were still in bed, asleep, and that this was truly the nightmare it seemed.

He watched Justin and Damon load the weapons and heard the metallic click-click as each one was cocked. The fearsome sound echoed in the silence of the new day. When Justin stepped forward to present the oblong leather case, Dominic made his selection swiftly, fatalistically, submitting his chosen weapon to a cursory examination. The pistols were his own, and had belonged to his father.

"Damon is as perplexed about this as you and I," Justin said, his breath hanging visibly in the frigid morning air. "Sir Algernon has hardly spoken a word to him—and Damon is his second! His forcing this duel upon you makes no sense."

"No," Dominic agreed, "but he left me no choice but to meet his challenge. I hope to heaven he doesn't mean this to be a killing affair, for I should hate to die without knowing the cause."

"Oh, there's no possibility of that," Justin replied, a little too heartily. "Depend upon it, he knows he's in the wrong, but daren't cry off for fear of being thought craven."

The twelve paces were duly marked out by the seconds, and the principals took their positions. Dominic, standing stiffly at attention, reflected that only yesterday he would have described himself as the most fortunate of fellows. He possessed a respected name, a title, a large fortune, a prosperous estate, good friends, and a cosy little mistress who adored him. But at that moment all of those advantages were as worthless as the dirt beneath his boots. On a duelling ground, all men met as equals.

"Take your marks!" Damon called out sharply, and the men raised their weapons.

Dominic, knowing that to fire into the air would be a confession of guilt, pointed the barrel of his pistol slightly to the left of the man who faced him.

"*Fire!*"

He heard the simultaneous, ear-splitting reports, then a sickening hiss when a bullet flew past his ear, coming so close that he felt the heat of it. The smell of singed powder filled his nostrils, and he knew he would relive that moment in his dreams for the remainder of his days. He was so surprised to find himself on his feet that for a moment he failed to realise that his antagonist had fallen, but as the clouds of grey smoke dissipated, he saw Sir Algernon seated on the grass, holding a balled-up handkerchief against his right thigh.

"Your father taught you to shoot better than that, boy," the baronet grunted when Dominic joined the others kneeling beside him.

"Yours taught you a damned sight too well," Dominic retorted grimly, fingering the cheek that might have been shattered a moment ago. "I swear I saw my life pass before me."

Lord Elston turned to the whey-faced surgeon hovering nearby and snapped, "Come here, damn you, and take a look."

As the young doctor fumbled with the clasp on his leather bag, his hand shook so badly that Justin Blythe asked in a rallying tone, "What, Master Sawbones, is this your first duel?"

To everyone's astonishment, the man nodded, and in a chilling dumb-show, he held his case open wide. It contained nothing more than a bandage or two, and a single probe. "Medical student," he choked.

"Damn you, Damon," Dominic thundered, "why didn't you engage an experienced surgeon?"

His friend's blue eyes blazed back at him. "How the devil was I to know the difference? He *told* me he was fully qualified." Wasting no more time on words, Lord Elston shrugged out of his fashionable, tight-fitting coat and fashioned a makeshift pillow, which he placed beneath Sir Algernon's head.

Dominic, eyeing the charred rent in the baronet's breeches, asked the nervous medical man if the ball could be extracted, and received a helpless look in reply. "Then we must return to town as quickly as possible. I trust he can sustain the journey?"

The medical student swallowed convulsively, his

prominent Adam's apple rising and falling. "Not if the artery was hit," he said in a voice of doom. "But if that were the case, he'd be nearly dead by now."

Dominic gave a snort of disgust.

As the young man bound his leg, Sir Algernon closed his eyes and murmured, "Best see to your safety, Nick, before the authorities hear about this."

"Nonsense, sir. You've got a scratch, nothing more, so how could I be in any danger?" he replied, with a certainty that was far from genuine.

The baronet squinted up at him. "I suspected she had a lover. Married her anyway, the more fool I, never guessing that you—Charles's son—would be the one to serve me such a trick." His face contorted in a spasm of pain that was as much mental as physical.

"Is *that* what this was all about?" Dominic asked in amazement. "Why didn't you say so? I swear, upon the honour you were so quick to doubt, that I never betrayed you. Why, you had only to ask Lady Titus, and you could have believed her denial."

"I dared not confront her—didn't want to hear lies, and couldn't bear to hear her say it was true."

Justin Blythe, his face filled with outrage, said staunchly, "Well, it's *not!* And anyone who said otherwise told you a base lie!"

"Base—yes, he is that indeed, if he knew of your innocence, Nick," the wounded man muttered cryptically. Looking up, he smiled and said, "This position is not only uncomfortable, but most undignified for someone of my advanced age. I'll thank you to get me home, lads."

The baron and the marquis made a chair of their crossed arms, and shifted Sir Algernon to the waiting coach. The drive to London was accomplished swiftly, and the baronet spoke only once, to ask Dominic, also riding in the carriage, if he knew any prayers. " 'I am the resurrection and the life, saith the Lord—' How goes the rest of it?''

" 'And whosoever liveth and believeth in me shall never die,' " Dominic recited woodenly.

"You should've been a parson," the older man said.

"Just now I rather wish I were a surgeon," he replied, and he was relieved when his friend gave a weak chuckle.

Immediately upon their arrival in Clifford Street, Sir Algernon was borne upstairs to his bed, to await the arrival of his personal physician. This gentleman answered the summons promptly, and Dominic, Justin, and Lord Elston remained on the premises to learn his opinion of the patient's condition. An hour passed with no word from the sickroom, and their optimism began to wane.

When Lady Titus herself entered the saloon, her face streaked with tears, it vanished altogether. Moving as stiffly as an old woman, she walked up to Dominic.

"*Why* did the doctor insist upon his being bled," she asked desperately, "when he had lost so much blood already?" Georgiana continued to gaze up at him, her eyes wide and blank with shock, and he sought in vain for something to say, some word of comfort—of apology. "At least he did not die thinking that we—you and I—" He put his arms around her, and she wept upon his shoulder, murmuring self-recriminations, all of which indicated that her husband's suspicions about her infidelity had not been unfounded. Dominic, conscious of the presence of Justin and Lord Elston, asked no questions, although he was curious about the identity of her lover.

It was his duty to prepare her for what lay ahead. Leading her to the sofa, he said gently, "You must steel yourself for the ordeal of an inquest, Georgiana. There were witnesses to the duel, and they will be called in to give evidence. We cannot hope to hush up the truth of how Sir Algernon received his wound.''

''I think he was more concerned for your welfare than his own,'' she whispered, dabbing at her streaming eyes with her handkerchief. ''He was so very careful to say nothing that might incriminate you. But you are not to blame—it was the doctor who killed him, Nick. The ball had to be extracted, but Algy ought never to have been bled—but for that, he would be alive still, and laughing with us now.''

Georgiana and Dominic, united by a shared grief and guilt, clasped hands, and silence fell in the very room where, only hours before, the whole tragedy had been set in motion.

2

IT WAS MIDNIGHT when Dominic reached St. Albans, some twenty miles to the north of London. Over the long, barren stretches of road he had spurred Lord Elston's horse as though the devil followed him, but he'd been careful to pass through villages at a leisurely, sedate pace to avoid attracting notice. Dead tired from lack of sleep and hours in the saddle, he cared not how this endless day ended, so long as it ended soon.

From force of habit he stopped at the White Hart, one of the several posting inns in the town. "You'll have no luck here, your honour," the ostler called out to him, "and none at the Woolpack, nor the Peahen either. 'Tis fair-day tomorrow, and not a bed to be had anywhere I know of."

"No matter," Dominic replied, "I merely require stabling for my horse." He dismounted and slung his saddlebags across his shoulder. Addressing the ostler once more, he said, "I hope your barn is not as full as your inn."

The fellow gave him a gap-toothed grin. "Nay, we've accommodation aplenty for beasts. 'Twill cost you five shillings."

Dominic handed over the requested sum with a curt reminder to rub the horse down properly. "One of Lord Elston's grooms will collect him tomorrow or the next day," he said before leaving the inn yard on foot.

Most of the houses on Holywell Hill were dark and silent, so he was surprised to see a light shining in an upstairs window of the one he sought. The maidservant who answered his knock gasped to find him on the doorstep, but he merely said, "Is your mistress yet awake?"

"Oh, aye." The girl continued to stare at him.

"Will you fetch her?"

But this lady, having heard the slight commotion, was already coming down the stairs, clad in her dressing gown. When the servant stepped aside to reveal the late-night visitor, she hurried down the last few steps and said briskly, "Find the decanter, Molly, and then go up and ready the spare bedchamber. Don't stand there gaping, now, but be quick about your business!"

As the girl scurried off, Dominic smiled fondly down at the diminutive, decisive mistress of the house. "What presumption, Cat Durham! I haven't yet asked you if I might spend the night."

"I should hope you know it isn't necessary for you to ask," she answered. "Come and sit down, my lord. You look ready to drop." Her hasty, all-encompassing glance at his pale, unshaven face took in the volumes of trouble writ there, and when she took the dark cloak from him, she noted the wealth of road dust upon it.

Dominic followed the lady into the parlour, and while she was busy lighting candles and stirring up the fire, he collapsed into an armchair, his every muscle throbbing with fatigue. When she asked if he had ridden all the way from London, he looked up at her curiously, blankly. He closed his eyes a moment to clear them, then rasped, "I had to. I fought a duel yesterday morning. Only yesterday?" he wondered aloud.

"Dear heaven," the lady whispered.

"Fortune did not favour my opponent. Nor me, though I still live."

Only a flutter of Cat Durham's eyelashes betrayed her distress over this chilling announcement. With seemingly unruffled composure she went to take the tray from Molly and reiterated her earlier command about preparing a room for his lordship. When the girl was gone, Cat poured out the wine and asked Dominic if he desired any food.

"Thank you, no." He accepted the glass she held out to him and leaned his head against the back of the chair. "It was Sir Algernon Titus who called me out," he told her. "We met at Chalk Farm, at dawn. But I never meant to kill him."

"Of course you didn't." Cat sat down, folding her hands in her lap. "And you needn't say another word about it if you'd rather not."

"I *must* talk of it, or go mad. He meant to kill me and missed—I wanted to miss him but didn't. I aimed well to the right of him, I'm sure of it, but the damned pistol threw left and I wounded him in the leg. Dear God, Cat, how he bled." He set his glass down and placed his black head between his hands.

"Why would Sir Algernon want to kill you?"

"Someone, I know not who, told him I was Georgiana's lover. I have no enemy, none that I know of, and I can't think why someone would wish to blacken my name. Unless it was the guilty party himself, seeking to put Algy off the scent. Or out of the way," he added grimly. "I daresay I'll never know the truth of it." He paused for another swallow of wine, then went on with his tale. "The attending surgeon was no surgeon at all, and Algy's physician was no better."

"But if *you* did not kill him," Cat said softly, "why should you have to flee?"

"Because there was an inquest this morning, and the damned medical man—the one who witnessed the duel—gave his evidence. It must have been damning indeed, for the jury returned a verdict of murder, Cat—willful murder!''

"But a score of duels are fought every year, some of them fatal, and the whole world looks the other way," she protested. "Mr. Best was never prosecuted after his affair with poor Lord Camelford, and even though Captain Macnamara was tried for killing Colonel Montgomery, he was acquitted. Why should your case be any different?"

"I don't know," he said. "But Damon took the precaution of hurrying me into hiding, and I spent the night at my cousin's rooms near Lincoln's Inn. Well before noon today the street-criers were shouting the inquest verdict for the whole world to hear. After sundown I left Justin's lodging house by a back way, and Damon, plucky lad, let me have one of his best horses and accompanied me to the edge of town. I trust he'll get some sort of message to Ellen. I felt rather like Charles the Second, begging him to look after her. 'Let not poor Nelly starve.' '' Dominic's mouth twisted. "That sort of gallantry seems to run in our family. My father said much the same thing to me, before he died. About you."

He was silenced by the thought that he might never see Ellen Cleary again. It was impossible not to think of her in the presence of the lady seated across from him, for all his mistresses had been chosen for their resemblance to Cat Durham—small, cuddly women, with dark hair and good sense and impeccable manners. Ellen, formerly a milliner's apprentice, was a merry, bright-eyed little thing, who had proved surprisingly loyal in the face of numerous rival propositions. He'd set her up in a modest house just off Picadilly, where he visited her regularly whenever he was in town. She'd have no difficulty finding a new protector, for if she wasn't exactly a beauty, she possessed qualities that were far more lasting, and which would serve her much better in the years ahead.

"However did you escape London undetected?" Cat wanted to know. "The keepers must have been on the watch at the Hyde Park gate, and beyond."

"It was the easiest thing in the world. My dear Cat, don't you know that Baron Blythe is 'a great rich fellow what drives about in a shiny coach with a crest on the door'? I heard him described to me in those very words." He ran his hand across a cheek shadowed with stubble and gave her a crooked grin. "Tonight, at each of the five toll gates between London and here, not a one of the keepers recognised his lordship. Would you have done?"

"No, and I certainly don't now," said Cat, smiling faintly. "In the morning I'll have to send Molly out to acquire a razor for you, and I hope she and I can manage to brush that coat into a semblance of its former self. But for now, if you will pardon my saying so, you ought to go up to bed, my lord."

Dominic, more than willing to heed this practical suggestion, made his way to the chamber allotted to him. A nightshirt had been laid out—he supposed it had belonged to his father, whose portrait stared down at him from the wall. Hoping it was merely a trick of the light that was responsible for that uncharacteristically stern expression in the painted eyes, he shed his clothes, slid the crisp shirt over his head, and climbed into bed. It had been forever since he'd slept. The night before the duel he had been wakeful, his nerves on edge, and last night had been even worse. But weary though he was, he still found it difficult to drop off to sleep, for whenever he closed his eyes, he saw the painful visions that had lingered in his mind for so many desperate hours: Sir Algernon lying on the grass, Justin's worried eyes, Damon's frown of concern, Georgiana's tear-streaked face. To banish these shades, Dominic stared up at the tester above his head, tried to conjure up Ellen Cleary's image, but it was even more elusive than slumber.

He woke several hours later, feeling somewhat refreshed. Upon discovering that his garments had been spirited away in the night, he covered himself with the dressing gown left in their place. The girl Molly brought him some shaving water and a shiny new razor, along with the news that her mistress had left the house on an errand. Then she hurried downstairs to fetch his breakfast, which came in the welcome form of sausages, fresh buns, and strong coffee. His long sleep, more or less restful, and the comfort of hot food combined to raise his spirits. As he ate, he wondered if perhaps his flight from London had been premature.

But when he said as much to his hostess upon her return, she was violently opposed to his plan to return to town. "You *can't* go back! Why, you might be taken up and put into prison!" Cat cried, her tiny hands fluttering in agitation. "It would be folly—only wait till I tell you what I've heard this morning."

Guessing a great deal from her face, so puckered with worry, he heaved a sigh. "It's hardly likely that pleasant news would have travelled so swiftly. What is being said?"

"That Lord Blythe will be sought by the law officers in a case of willful murder," Cat reported, holding out a folded newssheet. "I had this from the White Hart; a traveller up from London left it behind yesterday."

Dominic glanced at the column indicated by her trembling finger, which told him—and anyone else who chose to read it—the results of the inquest into the death of Sir Algernon Titus. It was a shock to see his own name in print, and to read of his alleged connexion with a vile crime of passion, as the duel was described. He laid the paper aside with a sinking heart, but he said with tolerable unconcern, "If these print-ers mean to whip the public into a frenzy by sensa-tionalising what has happened, I suppose I must remain here indefinitely."

Cat shook her head in protest. "That would be just as dangerous as returning to town. Not that I wouldn't be most happy to keep you," she faltered when he turned surprised eyes upon her. "But St. Albans lies directly on the London Road, so you'd hardly be safe for very long. Why, the landlord at the inn told me Bow Street Runners may be on the case already, and I daresay they'll be watching for you at the ports as well."

"If I must be wary of both land and sea, where can I go?"

"To Ireland."

"Ireland?" he said incredulously.

"Consider for a moment—you require no passport to get there, yet you'd be well beyond the reach of the London authorities. You may take my valise, and Molly has already gone to purchase some shirts for you. Now do listen carefully, Nick, for if you but—" Suddenly she broke off, flushing, and said in a sub-dued voice, "Your pardon, my lord."

He reached for one of her plump hands and squeezed it. "Don't be a goose, Cat. Hearing you call me Nick makes me feel a youth again." Her eyes darted to-wards the portrait of the first Baron Blythe, and he asked softly, "Haven't been pining for him, have you? He wouldn't approve of that, you know."

Cat crossed to the window to draw back the cur-tains. "Not pining," she said, "though I still miss him, and always shall. In London, during those first months without him, I was quite miserable. But last winter, after I came to St. Albans, I managed to find a sort of peace. I pass for a respectable widow, you see, and not a soul would ever guess quiet Mrs. Durham was once a nobleman's fancy-piece.''

Dominic regarded her bowed head, dappled with sunlight, and saw that the dark, neat chignon was beginning to show streaks of grey. It had been a dozen years since his father had introduced him to Cat, when she had been thirty, his present age. Now she was all of two-and-forty, and suddenly he felt even older than that.

"I have a favour to ask of you," he said, and she looked around. "Before I went into hiding, I did as Damon suggested and withdrew a substantial sum from my bank. I have it with me now, in large notes, and I want to leave—" he thought for a moment. "—a thousand pounds with you."

Her eyes flashed as she said, "Your father provided for me, and I lack nothing."

Laughing, Dominic shook his head at her. "Pull in your claws, dear Cat, the money isn't for you. But I do want you to put it with your own bankers against the time I have need of it. Will you?" After she nodded, he returned to the subject of his impending journey. "Now tell me, where do I pick up the Irish Road?"

"At Northampton. It's a busy enough place, so nobody will much notice a plain-dressed man. How will you travel?"

"It will be wiser, to say nothing of more comfortable, to go to Holyhead by post-chaise, and in slow stages. The longer I take to reach the port, the more relaxed the watches will be by the time I arrive there. It shouldn't be too difficult to engage a private fishing vessel to carry me across the channel to Ireland."

When this and other details of his trip had been settled, Cat told Dominic she would be sorry to see him go, although she knew he must, and soon. "When will you depart?"

"That depends entirely upon you, my dear Mrs. Durham," his lordship declared, "for until you return my breeches to me, I can go no farther than this room!"

Worried as she was, Cat was not immune to the charm of his smile, and she gave him one in exchange before rushing out of the room to do his bidding.

Dominic shifted on the hard, wooden seat, wincing as his stiffened muscles protested. He had chosen this bench not from a desire to torture his aching body any further, but because it commanded a view of the main road connecting Northampton to London. Thus far he had recognised none of the private carriages passing by, nor had he heard any report of Bow Street Runners in the neighborhood. Still, it was troubling, the fact that the only chaise available for hire was damaged, but not, he hoped, beyond repair. Even now the wheelwright was busy with what he trusted were the finishing touches to the rim.

Fortunately for him the Angel was all but deserted, and thus far only two other persons had stopped there, a young couple in a gig. Although the lady wore a white veil pinned to her bonnet, they were not newlyweds, as Dominic had originally supposed, for they were now bidding each other farewell. All he could see of the young woman was her slim, straight back, but he could hear her pleasant voice; it was neither shrinking nor shrill, the two things he most deplored in females. And his ear caught the warm undercurrent of humour when she told her friend, "You leave me in good hands, John, for Papa always used to say Mr. Gudgeon keeps the best cellar in Northampton. Now do not make such a disapproving face—I give you my word that I won't set foot in the taproom, or talk to strangers, or do anything shocking. I shall behave like a *proper* young lady."

Her companion threw back his head and laughed out loud. "Now *that* I should like to see!" He turned to climb the gig, but the lady placed a hand on his arm to stay him.

"Wait, John." Dominic saw her reach into her reticule, from which she extracted a banknote. "It's ten pounds," he heard her say, "and I wish it were ten times that. Will you send it to Lucy for me? She's at her mother's house, in Chelsea—Andrew can give you the precise direction." She bowed her head, and Dominic leaned forward, listening even more intently. "Samuel grows so fast now that he's rising two, and I must do what I can to keep him in dresses. I daresay he is too young to miss me much, but that's cold comfort."

"There now," the young man said, "did you not tell me, but a little while ago, that everything has happened for the best?" He clasped her hand, then took his place in the gig. As she looked up at him, the lace veil rippled and danced on the breeze. "Have a safe journey, my dear, and may God be with you."

The young woman stood in the yard, watching until he was gone, and as soon as she turned towards the inn, she reached up to adjust her veil. In the instant before that lacy curtain fell, Dominic received a brief, tantalising glimpse of her face, and climbed to his feet in polite acknowledgement of a female presence. She gave him a perfunctory nod in return as she swept past him to enter the building.

He concluded that she must be a married lady who had been unfaithful to her husband, and the child she'd mentioned had to be the result of her indiscretions. No doubt her spouse was unwilling to accept it as his, so she had been obliged to place little Samuel in the care of another woman, the Lucy who lived in Chelsea. Thinking over all he had observed and overheard, Dominic doubted that the fair-haired young man was her lover; he had seen nothing of illicit passion in their exchange, but friendship and brotherly concern.

The lady's sorrow over the separation from her young son haunted him. Ironic, he thought, as darkness fell upon the inn yard, that her shame was bringing a new life into the world, while his had been contributing to the loss of a life. He felt a strange bond with her, his fellow traveller on the road of adversity, for she was apparently as much a victim of cruel fate as he was.

At last the wheelwright put aside his tools, and a bow-legged ostler stumped towards the stables to ready the horses. Dominic, still curious about the lady, called him over and asked if he knew her. "Aye," the man replied, bobbing his head, "I've seen her often. Her father, the Capting, did abide over to Olney-way. So fond of her he was, she being his only chick. Miss was going to be wed next month, but from the looks of things, summat went awry." The ostler's mouth twisted to one side as he surmised, " 'Tis likely she shied off at the thought of the widow Hudgins as her mother-in-law. That one has a face could curdle new milk."

A single lady, Dominic sighed to himself, drawing his cloak around him to ward off the chill, and yet she was a mother. Had her shameful past driven her from her home? If so, she, too, was an outcast—hard enough for a man to bear, but for a woman even worse.

As Dominic considered her plight, his sympathy for her increased.

"I'm sorry, miss," the proprietor of the Angel told the young woman when she expressed her wish to hire a post-chaise for her journey to Staffordshire. "I've but one on the premises, with a broken wheel, and 'tis spoken for already. And though I'm expecting another back from Daventry, there's no saying when it will arrive. Or in what condition," he concluded gloomily.

Mr. Gudgeon, who so proudly advertised his neat carriages, fast horses, and experienced postilions, disliked turning people away, but owing to a sudden and unexpected demand, his coach house was nearly empty.

Unwelcome as these tidings were to her, the lady in the blue pelisse accepted them stoically. "So be it," she said. "I will not take my custom elsewhere—my father would turn in his grave, he was that loyal to the Angel. I'll await the chaise from Daventry and hope for the best."

He ushered her into a private parlour, where a cheerful coal fire leaped and crackled in the grate. Pulling off her gloves, Nerissa warmed her hands, and the rest of her; her pelisse was more fashionable than serviceable, and the drive in the open gig had chilled her to the bone. When she asked the landlord if he could recommend an inn at Lutterworth, where she expected to pass the night, he gave a favourable account of the Denbigh Arms there. "And where might you be bound, Miss Newby?" he asked.

"For a village called Leek, in Staffordshire. I daresay you've never heard of it."

Mr. Gudgeon showed every sign of being hurt by her lack of faith. "I fancy I knows most towns along the great roads, miss, being as how my postboys always return with some sad tale: a wheel come off at Ashborn, the traces broke at Towcester." He shook his head dolefully.

Nerissa's laugh was muffled by her veil, and she said gaily, "I hope you receive no such dire report of my journey!"

The landlord made no reply, being distracted by the presence of the ostler, who stood in the hall. "What is it, Ned?" he asked impatiently.

"Begging your pardon, sir," said the man, "but I've come to deliver a message from the gentleman

outside. He bid me tell you he's giving up the chaise
to the miss—says he'll stop here for the night and take
up his journey to Ireland on the morrow.''

It was the best of all outcomes for Mr. Gudgeon:
Miss Newby, whose late parent had been a valued cus-
tomer, would not suffer a delay, and he had acquired
a paying guest, who would need a bed, a meal or two,
and plenty of drink before continuing on his way.

Nerissa, who had heard this exchange, instantly forgot her promise to John Hudgins about not speaking
to strangers. ''How very kind, to be sure. Ned, will
you ask the gentleman to come in? I'd like to thank
him.''

Her veil distorted her vision, but when her benefactor entered the parlour a few minutes later, she could
see he was tall and well-formed, with dark hair. He
carried a triangular cocked hat, many years out of the
mode, and wore a long black cloak flecked with mud
and road dust.

''You are most generous, sir,'' she said, going to
meet him, ''but I'm sorry to be the cause of so much
inconvenience to you.''

''A good night's sleep is hardly an inconvenience,
ma'am, and that is what I gain by letting you take the
chaise.''

His hoarseness instantly roused Nerissa's compas-
sion. He was ill, and she was depriving him of the
only available conveyance. ''Perhaps I can repay your
kindness in kind,'' she said, as the thought came to
her. ''Ned mentioned that you are bound for Ireland,
and Lutterworth, where I will stop the night, lies on
the Irish Road. It appears that we are travelling in
the same direction, so we might as well share the
chaise, don't you agree?''

''You are asking me to accompany you?'' he asked,
surprise making his still voice more uneven.

Nerissa had acted impulsively, and, she now feared,

unwisely. Mortified, she murmured, "I've shocked you."

"Not at all," he said politely.

"Well, I've rather shocked myself," she confessed, "but it would be foolish—and selfish—to be constrained by convention when I may be of some assistance to you."

The gentleman's face, so pale and strained, relaxed in a smile. "During our journey to Lutterworth, I'll strive not to give you any cause to regret your magnanimity," he said, thereby making plain his acceptance of her invitation.

3

As THE CHAISE rolled out of the inn yard and into the night, Nerissa wondered if she had not made a grave mistake in so recklessly suggesting that the gentleman travel with her. She had thrust herself into a situation fraught with impropriety, and now she sat in a darkened carriage bound for an unknown town on an unfamiliar road, a stranger at her side—and a male one at that—and she had no one to blame for it but herself. But for twenty-three years impulse had been an ingrained habit, so much so that her father had often teased her about her fatal tendency to tumble headlong into trouble. Except that lately the troubles had not been very amusing ones, and at the present moment they lay heavy on her heart and mind.

It had been a long time since she had covered any distance greater than that between London and Olney, and never before had she gone anywhere by herself. But after the indignity and disgrace she had suffered in recent weeks, she doubted that travelling without a chaperone could further damage her reputation. At least, Nerissa told herself, she could take comfort from the fact that her travelling companion knew nothing about her other than her destination, and that she was paying a visit to a friend from her boarding school days.

Initially their discourse consisted of each enquiring whether the other was tolerably comfortable. He exhibited the sort of quiet good manners that would have soothed her alarms, had she been of a nervous disposition. Inevitably an awkward silence fell, with every sign of becoming a lasting one. Frantically, Nerissa searched her mind for some unexceptionable remark that would serve to inaugurate a dialogue between them. Before she could utter a syllable, the gentleman said quietly, in that curiously rough-edged voice, "You needn't be afraid of me."

Her head swerved in his direction. "I'm not."

"Yet you keep your face concealed." He sighed, as though disappointed. "I do understand, however, if our paths should ever cross again, you wouldn't want me to recognise you as the lady I escorted to Lutterworth in a closed carriage at night."

Behind her veil, Nerissa smiled. "No, I certainly would not."

"Do not feel you must tell me your name," he went on, "for your safety is ensured by your anonymity. As is mine," he added grimly, under his breath.

She suspected him of jesting with her, perhaps to put her at ease, so she asked merrily, "Are you in such grave danger, then?"

"If you only knew . . . the tales of my exploits might alarm even so intrepid a lady as you appear to be," he replied in a lighter tone.

"Now I don't know what to believe, for a moment ago you said I need not fear you," she reminded him.

"Well, I've only recently become a reformed character."

Laughing softly, Nerissa made a slight adjustment to the lap robe. At that moment the wheels met with an uneven patch of the road, and both passengers reached up to take hold of the leather straps provided for just such an occurrence. Although Nerissa gripped hers tightly, she couldn't avoid jostling the gentleman. "I'm sorry," she murmured, blushing in the darkness.

Once they were past the rough spot, he said, "I'd forgotten how tiresome night travel can be."

Although Nerissa agreed with him, she ventured the opinion that daytime travel was not much different. "For even if the postilions can see the ruts in their path, they don't always manage to circumvent them."

They fell into an easy discussion of the many perils of travel. The gentleman described a particularly wild drive from Bath to London, attended by such mishaps as a drunken coachman, a broken wheel, and a tumble into the road. When he reached the end of his tale, he laughed, which made him look much younger, and even more handsome. Nerissa regretted that it was so dark inside the coach, and her vision was so impaired by her veil.

He offered no explanation whatever for his journey to Ireland. She assumed that he had property there, or family. Or, she thought, eyeing the old-fashioned cocked hat that lay on the seat between them, he might have suffered financial reverses and could be escaping his creditors. His dark cloak and the doeskin riding breeches were well-made, although somewhat the worse for travel stains. And the black boots, though sadly dulled by dust, were the most expensive kind. She knew, because her father had owned just such a pair.

The memory of that similarly tall, dark gentleman was always with her; his loss was an unhealed slash upon her heart. As a child, she had been accustomed to his extended but temporary absences, and yet as a grown woman she was quite unable to accept the permanence of his death. She had never admitted to her intrepid parent that old fear from her childhood, that he might not return from one of his voyages. That he could die of a fever in the prime of his life, in a sickroom with a doctor in attendance, had seemed such a remote possibility that she had never even considered it. She missed his hearty embrace and lively discourse, spiced with tales of the exotic places where he had traded—Madras and Calcutta, China and the islands of the West Indies. But most of all she missed the way his eyes, the same deep blue as her own, had filled with pride whenever they had gazed at her.

People had frequently commented upon how closely she resembled him. But one of Nerissa's treasures was a miniature portrait of her mother, a beauty from the island of Jersey, which showed quite plainly the origins of her milky complexion and the reddish tints in her unruly chestnut mane. Still, her papa's legacies were the more obvious ones: the indigo eyes and slanting dark brows, the humourous curve of her lips, and her low, rich laugh. The beauty mark hovering near her mouth came from neither parent and it was entirely her own.

Six months had passed since Captain Richard Newby had been laid to rest in Olney churchyard, beside his wife and sister. Not long ago Nerissa had believed herself incapable of straying very far from that grassy, well-tended grave, or the fields she and her papa had roamed. He had left her in Olney, and there she had intended to remain, almost as if he might return to her, and her reluctance to uproot herself had been so strong that she had not discouraged Andrew Hudgins when he'd hinted that he hoped to marry her when the prescribed period of her strictest mourning ran its course. But her hopes for a happy future at his side, one that would be ordered and ordinary, had been shattered by the gossip linking her to little Samuel. Less than a month after her father's demise, when the people of Olney had begun to whisper about her relationship to the baseborn child, she'd believed the talk would die down in time. Unchecked, it had spread like some evil, destructive disease, touching and tainting everyone connected with her, especially poor Andrew.

Nerissa hadn't lacked a safe haven from the tempest that had forced her from her home. Her mother's family, the de Tourzels, still lived on that remote isle so uncomfortably close to the Continent. But they were complete strangers, only names to her, so in the end she had struck them off her list. Her father's cousin, a wealthy and powerful duke, was someone she knew very well indeed, quite well enough to know what would happen if she should seek shelter in his elegant mansion in Mayfair. She would be obliged to submit to a tediously formal introduction to society, at her relation's expense; even worse, everyone would expect her to apologise for her father's mercantile interests and activities, and that she could never do. There were times, and this was one of them, when the comfort and commiseration of a friend would be preferable to any kindness from a relative, however well meaning. And she had therefore dispatched a letter to Laura Sedgewick, *née* Greene, announcing her impending visit.

As the chaise lumbered on towards she knew not what, Nerissa began to feel the first faint stirrings of optimism. She was strong and healthy, she had money enough, and she was leaving her past and her troubles farther behind with every milepost she passed.

The yard of the many-gabled Denbigh Arms in Lutterworth, the inn so highly recommended by Mr. Gudgeon of the Angel, was cluttered with coaches, ostlers, and postboys, which seemed to prove its popularity with travellers along the Holyhead Road. As the gentleman handed her out of the carriage, Nerissa prayed it had rooms enough to accommodate two more.

When her companion turned away to supervise the removal of their baggage from the rear of the vehicle, she pondered how best to raise the sensitive subject of who should pay the posting charges. The notion of being beholden to a stranger was abhorrent to her, yet she hesitated to press money upon him for fear of offending him. His single, battered valise more than hinted that he could be short of cash.

Her uncertainty must have been apparent to him, because he said firmly, "You may go inside, ma'am. I shall settle with the postboy."

"Might we not share the expense?" She received no reply, for he was staring beyond her, and his expression of grave concern made her glance over her shoulder. The object of his scrutiny was a short, burly man in a frieze coat who stood in the side-yard talking to one of the ostlers. His accent and mode of speech, barely audible to her, proclaimed him a resident of one of London's less refined boroughs.

The gentleman grasped Nerissa's wrist, and said, in a wild, rough whisper, "I need your help. A matter of life or death—my life, or my death!"

His urgency startled her, but her response was immediate. "Yes, of course, what shall I do?"

"Keep your veil lowered, and remain silent, no matter what I might say," he instructed. "I swear no harm will come to you."

He flung one arm around her waist, and she stifled the sharp protest that rose instinctively to her lips. He hurried to the door, and the moment they crossed the threshold, he began shouting for the landlord at the top of his voice. This was puzzling; a moment before he'd been so anxious to avoid attracting notice. The common room was filled with men, all staring curiously at the noisy intruder, and Nerissa was thankful her face was still hidden by the veil.

A neatly dressed man stepped forward. "How may I be of service to you, sir?" he asked.

With a harsh laugh, the gentleman tightened his hold on Nerissa and said, "Is it not obvious? Show us to a bedchamber, man, and let it be your best!"

The landlord hesitated before replying, "I've but one room left, by no means my finest."

" 'Twill suffice—so long as it has a bed."

Although Nerissa was willing to lend him the assistance he required, she felt this was going too far. But he had told her to keep quiet, so she indicated her objection by tugging upon his sleeve.

"So impatient, sweetheart?" he cried, grinning down at her. "But soon we'll be alone, and you'll have me all to yourself!"

An expression of distaste crossed the landlord's face and he said stiffly, "Follow me, sir, if it please you."

Nerissa's companion let him precede them up the narrow staircase, and when the man's back was turned, he whispered in her ear, "Good girl! Don't fail me now, I beg you." He pretended to stumble on the stairs, recovering just in time to prevent a fall, and smiled sheepishly up at the landlord. "I fear I've had an overabundance of spirits this night. But how could one avoid it, with such a lovely bride to toast?" He pinched Nerissa's waist, and she let out a horrified gasp.

"My felicitations, sir," said the landlord at his most wooden, from the upper landing. With a nod in Nerissa's direction he added, "And madam."

He ushered the amorous bridegroom and his veiled wife into the one available chamber, which was dominated by an enormous fourposter. It's other furnishings included a gate-legged table flanked by Windsor chairs and another pair of armchairs on opposite sides of the fireplace. Two servants carried the baggage into the room, and their master stirred the fire. He inquired politely whether Madam desired the maid's services. "I can send Nan up to you, if you wish."

Nerissa, who caught the trace of pity in his tone, had never needed it more. "Thank you, no, but I could fancy some supper," she announced in a shrinking voice that she hardly recognised as belonging to herself.

To her great surprise and relief, her escort endorsed this request. "An excellent notion, my love. We will dine. My good man, pray send up a bottle of your best vintage at once." He tossed his cape onto the bed, and the landlord bowed himself out of the room.

Nerissa removed her bonnet and veil while the gentleman crossed to the window and drew the curtains. "I *do* hope," she said with what she hoped was withering disdain, "you mean to tell me why we are playing this ridiculous May-game."

Dominic turned around, but his intended reply was a thing forgotten.

She was much younger than he had originally supposed, for the composure she had displayed throughout the journey had led him to estimate her age at something nearer his own. Her charming countenance, now clearly visible for the first time, caught him unawares. The lady's hair was a rich mahogany in colour, and she was gazing back at him with the largest, bluest eyes he'd ever seen, and she had a pair of full, rosy lips accentuated by a tiny black mole as dramatic and alluring as a courtesan's beauty patch. He understood perfectly why she'd been so careful to keep her face covered: having once seen it, no man could forget it.

"I'm not mad," he told her, never guessing that his bemused expression might encourage her to think otherwise. "Indeed, I am in grave danger."

"Who was that man outside?" she demanded. "Do you know him?"

"Not exactly. I've never seen him before, but he must know me. I will have been described to him." She was, he noted, taller than the average for her sex, and in addition to possessing a wanton's face, she had a superb figure, lithe and lush. Belatedly recalling her question, he said, "The man is a Bow Street Runner."

"Good heavens," she breathed and her eyes grew even larger, a thing he had not believed possible.

Drawing a chair forward, he indicated she should sit, which she did as swiftly as if her legs had suddenly given way. "We haven't much time to speak in private, I'm afraid, for they'll be bringing our dinner soon. I'm glad you thought of food—I'm hungry as the devil."

"I, too. But, sir, we cannot continue in this charade—"

"My name is Nick," he proceeded as though she hadn't spoken, "and because I cannot be forever calling you 'sweetheart' and 'my love' and so on, may I know yours?"

"Nerissa Newby. But, sir—"

"Forgive my boorishness on the staircase just now, Miss Newby, but you can understand why it was necessary. While we are alone together, I will refrain from crudities of that kind."

"You cannot expect to go on any further with this—this *hoax,*" she persisted, with ill-concealed impatience.

"But I must," he said evenly. "The moment we arrived here you became indispensable to me, for I am safe only as long as the Runner believes me to be an overeager bridegroom. Until he is gone, which may not be till morning, I have no intention of leaving this room—at least, not for any considerable period of time."

She gripped her hands together tightly, and her reply emerged as a nervous whisper. "You must know I will be ruined if I spend the night here with you."

"And I may die if you do not." Dominic added more gently, "All I'm asking is your permission to sleep on the floor. I will not otherwise impose upon you, on my word of honour."

"But there must be other inns in the town, other

towns on this road," she said desperately, not yet giving up her attempt to dissuade him.

"I prefer to remain beneath the same roof as the Runner, for to travel ahead of him would be to risk his catching up with me. I had much rather keep my eye on him for the present, and try to discover where he is bound."

Nerissa bounded up from her seat. "What have you done that he should be chasing after you?" Perhaps, she thought desperately, she had reason to be more frightened than she actually was.

A sharp knock sounded upon the door, and the gentleman took a single, swift step towards her. "I will tell you everything by and by."

Nerissa had divined the purpose of his advance, but she was not quick enough to evade him. His arms imprisoned her, and had he not held her so tightly, she believed she would have fallen to the floor from the shock of it. Firm, insistent lips smothered her startled gasp, and she was further alarmed to discover that his kiss sparked something more than outrage in her breast.

Suddenly, without warning, her captor released her. Vaguely aware that another person had entered the room, Nerissa looked towards the door, blushing furiously.

A pimply serving boy righted his tray just in time to prevent the full decanter and a pair of glasses from tipping to the floor. He deposited his burden on the table and mumbled, "Master says tell you dinner'll be brought in half an hour, sir."

Nerissa was grateful for his ill-concealed grin, because as soon as she recognised the humour of the situation, her fears about it subsided.

When she and the man she knew only as Nick were alone again, he poured the wine. "To a successful deception," he said, raising his glass.

Still somewhat ruffled by what had just transpired, she said tartly, "I wish you will not take my compliance for granted, sir—it's bad enough that you broke your word to me only seconds after giving it." He looked back at her curiously and she reminded him, "You promised not to impose yourself upon me, and if that display just now was not an imposition, then I don't know what is."

"It won't happen again. I understand your concerns, but—"

"Do you indeed?" she flared. "How *can* you, when I don't even know myself whether I'm on the point of being murdered, molested, or robbed by you, Mr.—Mr. whatever-your-name!"

"Oh, I'm not so fearsome as all that. Nor is it my habit to prey upon defenceless females, so you are quite safe from attack, Miss Newby. Besides, not even the most *ruthless* criminal would risk an outcry with a Bow Street Runner so near."

"You don't look like a criminal," she admitted, "although you've already proved that you are rather more than ruthless."

The ghost of a smile flickered across his pale face. "True, but I mean no harm, neither to your person nor your property."

"That's all very well," she retorted, "but you've already destroyed something less tangible, but no less valuable—my reputation."

"My dear girl, you aren't acquainted with a single soul in this inn, and no one but ourselves will ever know what does—or does not occur—in this room." Pausing, Dominic ran one hand through his black hair, then asked, "Do you truly believe the reputation of a lady is of greater value than the *life* of a gentleman?"

Nerissa, finding no answer to that question, sat down before the fire and submitted her wine glass to a close inspection.

"Yesterday, I fought a duel near London," he said, his voice flat, devoid of all expression. "You already know I am sought by the authorities, so you can guess the outcome."

She looked up. "You killed a man?"

"That point is open to dispute," he sighed. "Still, however you look at it, I am responsible for his death. But what makes it so much harder for me is that he was my friend."

It was a dreadful burden, and Nerissa, who had been so absorbed by her own problems that she hadn't even guessed his might be worse, suddenly felt ashamed.

"Miss Newby," he continued, "if you were as concerned about your reputation as you make out, you'd have a chaperone, or at the very least, a maidservant at your side."

The fire dancing in the grate was nothing compared to the sudden flame in Nerissa's cheek. She had to accept that it was useless to prose on about her good name, for her own words and actions had given him no reason to believe her. At some cost to her pride, she acknowledged, "You are perfectly correct, I have no respectability to sacrifice on your behalf. I am not a proper young woman, I never was. Or could be," she added softly, staring down at the fire. "And that is why I, too, am a fugitive. Neither am I a stranger to scandal, for we are old friends, indeed."

This time when he approached her, she didn't back away. After hours of sitting beside him in the carriage, and now that he had kissed her, his nearness was familiar to her, even comforting. She looked up at him without fear. His eyes, she noted, were grey, and the white skin surrounding them was etched with faint lines of weariness.

"Neither are you and I strangers, Nerissa," he said, and the husky, whisper-like words sent a shiver along her spine. "Despite the fact that we've been acquainted only a few hours, and though I know nothing about you but your name. I don't seek to uncover your secrets, and you already know the worst of mine. By revealing it, I have placed my very life in your hands. Can you guess why I did?''

She continued to gaze mutely back at him, and he explained, ''My every instinct tells me that I can trust you. Twice tonight your generosity of spirit has outweighed your concern for the finer points of convention. Otherwise you would not have offered me a place in the chaise, nor would you have accompanied me to this room. Be generous with me again, and I swear by all I hold dear that you will not suffer for it.''

His voice was curiously rough and smooth all at once, and so very persuasive. A strong current of communion surged through Nerissa, for she could accept the truth of his assertion that they were alike. If he was a strange creature, well, then, so was she. And what he said was quite true, no one in the world would ever know of this night's adventure. That being so, what danger could there be in it?

Even before she gave him her answer, he said softly, ''I thank you, Miss Newby, with all my heart.''

His uncanny ability to trace her thoughts even as they began to take shape in her mind confused and disturbed her, just as he did when, with infinite tenderness, he reached down to brush a stray lock of hair from her brow.

4

FULLY COMMITTED TO helping the gentleman, Nerissa abandoned her chair and knelt down before the small sea chest that still bore her father's initials in brass. "If I am to pass as your wife," she said over her shoulder, "I think I had better put on my mother's wedding band." She lifted the lid and took out the ivory box containing her valuables: a pearl necklet, a garnet set, and several rings.

When he asked if he might look at the box, she gave it to him, and he turned it this way and that, examining the intricate carving. "Very pretty," he said, returning it to her.

"Don't you mean to have a look inside?" she quizzed him.

"Thievery is not my crime, I told you that. Is it Chinese?"

"Yes. Papa had a habit of purchasing pretty trifles for me on his voyages—bits of ivory and jade from China, and sandalwood from India. He was captain of a merchant ship," she explained.

Dominic offered to refill her glass, but Nerissa declined, lest an excess of wine make her lose her reserve entirely. Not knowing what else to do with herself, she continued to unpack, a flush decorating her cheek as she removed such items of apparel as a bedgown and a lace-edged nightcap. She wished she could match her companion's easy acceptance of this unusual situation, but he was a man, she thought resentfully, and therefore could have no notion of how his very presence might discomfit a female.

She was arranging her silver-backed brush and mirror on the mantel when she heard footsteps in the passage.

"That will be our dinner," he said.

And so it was. This time the serving boy was accompanied by an older waiter, and after the two had opened up the gate-legged table, they proceeded to lay out a modest repast. The sight and aroma of roast duckling was most welcome; suddenly Nerissa was very hungry. She took the chair opposite her bridegroom-for-a-night, smiling at him in a spirit of camaraderie, and he smiled back. The lad snickered audibly and received a sharp rebuke from his superior. Throughout the ensuing meal, conversation was general, in part because of the presence of the servants, but also from Nerissa's fear that she might inadvertently slip out of her role.

When the covers were removed, the waiter placed a bottle of port on the table and asked if the gentleman required anything more. "Why, yes," he replied, "you may send my compliments to all the gentlemen in the taproom, and bid them enjoy a round at my expense."

The youth's eyes bulged upon hearing this, and his comrade said respectfully, "Aye, your worship."

Then the bridegroom pressed a handsome gratuity upon each of the servers, and the boy was emboldened to announce, "To be sure, sir, it's a famous night for the Denbigh Arms. There's a Bow Street Runner below, wishful of stopping the night here. It's my belief he's on a case, though he will not say outright."

"Cease your chatter, lad," the waiter warned him sharply. "New-wedded folk care naught for Runners."

"Oh, but we do." Dominic smiled at Nerissa, who nearly choked on her wine. "So, my love," he said brightly, "our wedding night will be memorable in at least one respect—we have the honour of sleeping at the same inn as a Bow Street Runner! My good man, let him have as many bottles as he pleases this night, and tell the tapster to add his charges to my reckoning."

The two servers exited, and when the cheerful sound of their laughter faded along the passage, Nerissa discovered that her own merry mood had vanished with them. Now that she was once more alone with the man named Nick, she felt as nervous as any true bride. Perched uncertainly on the edge of her chair, she fidgeted with a bowl of nuts and sweetmeats, picking out the almonds, and avoided his eye. She wondered what she would do if he tried to force himself upon her during the night. Would the servants, believing her to be his lawful wife, respond to her cries for help?

She wished she could believe he was no threat to her, but whenever she let herself remember the intensity of his kiss, and her own mad desire to respond, she was troubled. She conjured up the image of her mild, gentle suitor, who had never given her cause for alarm. How shocked Andrew would be if he ever knew she had spent a night with a stranger—and when she heard the stranger laugh softly, she realised she had spoken her thought aloud.

"You mustn't mention another fellow's name on your wedding night," he jested. "It will make your husband jealous. Is Andrew the unhappy swain you left behind, the one with a dragon of a mother?"

Nerissa's head jerked up. "Was Gudgeon gossiping about me this afternoon?"

"Not he. I had that tidbit from the ostler."

"Well," she said matter-of-factly, "I had several reasons for terminating my engagement to Mr. Hudgins, and his mother was but one of them. If I ever *do* marry, I think it will have to be to a gentleman who has no mother. Or sisters,'' she added darkly, remembering how spiteful the four Hudgins girls had sometimes been.

"We are well matched, you and I," he said with mock gravity. "Apart from an aunt I seldom see, I am quite unencumbered by female relations. As we are on the subject of family, how does it happen that yours permits you to jaunter about the country alone?''

"I haven't any family," she answered bluntly. "Which is why I must depend upon my friend to give me a home, for the present. She is wed to a solicitor, a very fine man, and they have three children.''

When her lovely face clouded over, Dominic supposed she must be thinking about another child—her own little Samuel. By way of a diversion, he said, "Have you always lived in Olney?''

"Only for the past two years, and during my childhood. I was at school for a time, and then with Papa in his house in the Adelphi Terrace. He liked to live as near to the water as he could, so we had a fine view of the Thames, but I was never partial to the situation—the stench at low tide!'' She wrinkled her nose expressively.

Dominic, aware that the Adelphi was no longer inhabited by persons of fashion, was now able to make an informed guess as to Miss Newby's precise social standing. She had more than hinted that her father had been involved in trade, which meant she sprang from merchant stock. Her origins must be respectable, but no more than that, and given the strict code of morality of the middle class, her relations had probably cast her off when she had gotten herself into trouble.

It was yet too early for bed. Remembering Cat Durham's insistence that an occasional game of patience would relieve the tedium of his lonely nights at remote, wayside inns, he asked Nerissa if she liked to play cards.

"Have you some?"

"I do." He went to fetch the pack Cat had put in his valise, and returned to the table. "Piquet is my preference. Shall I teach you?"

"My papa did so years ago," Nerissa replied. "But if you think me a pigeon ripe for plucking, you are much mistaken, sir. I have no intention of gaming away my funds."

"It's not your money I want, but a much higher stake." Dominic shuffled the pack expertly, leaving her to wonder at his meaning. When he had finished dealing the cards, he looked up to say, "I covet one of the feather pillows from your bed—the floor is cold and hard, you know!"

She joined in his laughter, and a moment later the contest began.

Although Nerissa's was the more comfortable accommodation that night, she was the wakeful one. Lying in the vast fourposter, listening to the deep breathing of the gentleman who reclined on a makeshift bed of blankets—and a pillow—she knew that he'd had no difficulty dropping off to sleep. She had to smile, remembering her fear that he might try to slip under her covers and have his way with her. He was too weary to attempt her seduction, and knowing what she now did about his recent history, she could understand it.

But she had also seen his face in that moment when she had revealed her face to him. His reaction hadn't surprised her, nor had it pleased her. Instead, it had reminded her that nearly all of her present sorrows could be traced to the one thing about herself that was beyond remedy or change—her appearance.

Even as a child she had been aware of being different. Not due to any excess of beauty, not in those days, but from what she had deemed a hopeless lack of it. As a result, she had developed an early rapport with adults; unlike her chief playmates, Ruth and Judith Hudgins, they didn't ridicule her too-large eyes, disfiguring black mole, and thick, unruly hair. Her greatest friend was her father, who fondly referred to her as his little gypsy girl, and she had dearly loved her Aunt Portia.

The gentle spinster, following her brother's instructions, had placed her spirited, precocious charge in a seminary for gentlemen's daughters. Happily incarcerated at her school, content with her lessons and her new friends, Nerissa quickly outgrew her self-consciousness. The uneventful years flew by, and one day she looked up from her books long enough to discover that many of her contemporaries were suffering the agonies of puppy fat and spots and crooked teeth. Miraculously, she was passing through adolescence unscathed. That dread sense of being different came rushing back, only this time, she was surprised to find that the difference was to her advantage. In her thirteenth year she was considered one of the two prettiest girls in her form, an honour that had followed with regularity during the succeeding terms. She found an ally and a friend in the other beauty, Laura Greene, an ethereal blonde. The two girls admired each other fervently; that they were also perfect foils physically did not occur to them until several years later. Nerissa, so tall and dark and wild, was a splendid contrast to Laura, who was small and fair and ladylike.

At about the time his daughter emerged from the schoolroom, Captain Newby abandoned the high seas and settled in London to manage his business affairs. Nerissa, suitably chaperoned by her aunt, met the many gentlemen who made up her father's curious and varied collection of friends: seamen and scholars, lords and lawyers, poets and priests. His reputation as an excellent host and raconteur, coupled with her provocative beauty, lured many a male visitor to the handsome house in the Adelphi Terrace.

Nerissa's figure, which had matured early and fully enough to make her the envy of her schoolmates, began to attract scrutiny of another kind. As a girl she had deplored her long legs, thinking them coltish, but as a young woman she learned to like the way they enabled her to keep up with a gentleman's stride. Her rippling chestnut hair would, if coaxed, hold a curl to perfection, and even the beauty mark, previously the bane of her existence, turned out to be an asset. She was not vain of her looks, merely conscious of them, like any handsome animal that knows itself to be remarkable and is frequently pointed out as such. This awareness showed in her gait, in the proud tilt of her dark head, and in the perceptive glint in her blue eyes.

In her father's drawing-room she met with startled, admiring glances; on the streets of London, she was the recipient of sly, sidewise stares. And it wasn't long before Miss Portia Newby began making noises about the necessity of presenting Nerissa to society in the proper fashion. Their cousin, the Duke of Solway, might lend his assistance—the happy fact that the heir to the dukedom was very near her niece's age had occurred to the good lady. But before any of her grandiose schemes for Nerissa's advancement could be put into action, she suffered a fatal heart spasm. Within the year, her brother the captain was also dead.

Nerissa, valiantly striving to shift her thoughts from the unhappy events of the past, rearranged her covers and turned on her side. Eventually she slept, fitfully but dreamlessly.

In the morning, she was roused by a knock upon the door. Lifting her head from her pillow, she discovered that the gentleman was gone, but his valise still stood in the corner and his coat hung from a peg on the wall. The insistent rap sounded once more, and although she would have preferred to tell the intruder to go away, she mumbled, "Come in."

It was a chambermaid, an ugly, gawking girl who bobbed an execrable curtsey, spilling a little of the water from the brass pitcher she carried. Nerissa watched her pour the rest of it into the washbasin, and the wispy curls of steam rose from the bowl so invitingly that she thrust the covers aside. "Where is Mr.— where is my husband?" she asked.

"Bein' shaved," the girl replied. "Should I iron somethin' out while you're washin'?"

This was not necessary, for Nerissa had packed her trunks carefully, guarding her garments against creases with paper. She changed into a fawn-coloured muslin gown, and when she sat down at the table and held up her silver-backed hand mirror, she decided that the snowy ruffle at her throat lent her an appropriately matronly appearance.

"Let me arrange your hair for you, ma'am," the girl offered.

It was soon evident to Nerissa that her eager handmaid had little experience in the art of hairdressing. She suffered the pulling and tugging of her tresses without a murmur, but when the brush hit her temple for the second time, she thanked the girl with more politeness than was warranted, saying, "You may fetch the bottle of scent I left on the washstand."

Even this simple task was too much for the clumsy maid. She dropped the delicate crystal vial, shattering it and spilling the contents on the floor. Nerissa, barely keeping a rein on her impatience, bade her clean up the shards of glass. When this was accomplished, she said dismissively, "Thank you, that will be all," and the red-faced servant girl fled, nearly colliding with the gentleman.

He was clad in shirt, waistcoat, and breeches, with his cravat neatly tied and his cuffs buttoned. "Good morning, Madam Wife." He sniffed the air, now oppressively scented with roses. "A heady perfume."

"And an expensive one," she said mournfully. "Now I shall have to make do with lavender water." As she pinned the final coil of hair into place, she asked if it was safe for him to be wandering about the inn.

"Oh, the Bow Street Runner is long gone," he said, shrugging into his coat. "I was a joyful witness to his departure, and the moment he was out of the way, I made the arrangements for our journey to Leek."

Startled, she asked, "What do you mean, *our* journey?"

"I'm escorting you there, of course." Nerissa opened her mouth to protest, but he forestalled her, saying, "Now let's not begin this day as we ended the last one, with a catalogue of objections. The landlord tells me that Leek is on the road to Holyhead and as I happen to be bound for Ireland, your destination lies directly in my path."

Nerissa, sadly out of temper after her restless night and the annoyances of the morning, said sharply, "Is this offer prompted by chivalry—or convenience?"

"Both," he answered imperturbably. "I did hope I might continue to pose as your bridegroom for the distance of sixty or seventy miles."

Although she frowned, it was not in response to what he had said. "You've a cut on your cheek," she told him, and handed him her mirror.

"So I have," he agreed. "I'm afraid the barber who attended me is not the most skilled I've ever encountered." After she had recounted the whole of her experience with the hapless chambermaid, he smiled at her and said, "Poor Miss Newby, no wonder you're out of sorts! Now tell me, may I accompany you for the remainder of your journey?''

"Only if you will tell me your surname," she said spiritedly, "for you still have the advantage of me in that respect."

"It is Blythe." Dominic's trust in her was such that he would have admitted the existence of his title as well, had he not been afraid of endangering her. If the Runner did succeed in tracing him, his lovely accomplice would be placed in a precarious position; only by leaving her in ignorance of his exact identity could he ensure her safety. So he invented an alias for himself, albeit one that was founded upon truth, and rechristened himself when he announced, "I am Nick Blythe, Esquire."

The chaise into which he duly handed his supposed bride was not so new as the one Mr. Gudgeon of the Angel had provided, but it was no less comfortable. The postboy was a stunted, stupid fellow, but apparently he understood his passengers' desire to make short work of their journey; he spurred his horses indefatigably along the miles of open road, past fields and towns and the occasional manufactory. As the day wore on, Nick grew more and more optimistic about his chances of eluding the authorities.

Nerissa Newby, whom Providence had placed in his hands, was an entertaining companion, and easily entertained; his gratitude warmed into genuine liking. He encouraged her to talk about herself, and by careful questioning he was able to learn something of her history—her early years with her aunt in Olney, her days at school, and her later life in London. Knowing the shame of her past as he already did, he could see that her fall from grace had been inevitable, even inescapable. He sympathised with her, for with that sea-dog of a father, and no mother to guide and rear her properly, how could she have avoided being the prey of

some unscrupulous gentleman? And what a tempting
piece she was altogether, with her provocative face
and that voluptuous figure. Sitting so near to her, in
such a confined space, he was inclined to regret that
a man of honour must not trifle with a damsel in distress, however beautiful and available and unpro-
tected.

Although she never once alluded to her disgrace, or
her baby son, everything she said confirmed his belief
that these were responsible for her rift with her Mr.
Hudgins. The more he knew of her, the more he believed she had confessed the truth to her fiance, only
to be rewarded for her honesty by repudiation and banishment. Nick supposed he would never discover exactly what had happened in Olney, and it was not
something he could ask; he had to respect her reserve
as she respected his.

The late Captain Newby had taught his daughter far
more than the surprising proficiency at piquet she had
displayed the previous night. She was knowledgeable
about current political events and was particularly well
versed in the various naval campaigns of recent years.
But as much as he enjoyed her lively style of conversation, such heavy topics as politics and war grew bur-
densome after a while.

She must have felt the same, because at one point
she said, ''Mr. Blythe, last night you bested me in a
game of skill. I wonder if you are brave enough to put
sheer luck to the test, and join in a game of travelling
piquet?''

Nick hadn't played since his childhood, so he pre-
vailed upon her to refresh his memory. With painstaking care she explained the various point values, and
when she was done he observed that since it was such
a blustery day, he placed no dependence on seeing a
person riding a grey horse, or an old woman under a
hedge.

"Craven," she murmured.

"Yet a few miles back I saw a gig carrying a man and a woman and a child, so that nets me forty points at the start."

"Unfair! We hadn't yet begun to play," she protested. "The game will commence as soon as we reach the next mile-post."

For the next two hours they kept their noses pressed to their respective windows, each crying out with delight when some meaningful object came into view. They had no paper and pencil and thus had to add their scores in their heads; the sport was enlivened by disputes over the accuracy of the total.

"Three hundred and sixty-five," Nerissa announced, when at last they called a halt.

"Two hundred ninety-seven," was Nick's grudging admission. "How came you to do so well at the last? I demand a strict account, ma'am, and a refusal will confirm my belief that I've been cheated."

"Sixteen flocks of sheep at twenty points, two flocks of geese at ten, nine men on horseback for a total of eighteen points, and seven persons walking along the road at one point apiece. That's the tally and I stand by it."

"Are you quite certain about the sixteen flocks of sheep?"

"I am," she stated firmly. "There's an advantage to sitting on this side of the carriage, you know. Being on the traffic side, you will have seen more post-chaises and horsemen."

"Six chaises, eleven men on horseback. Perhaps we should continue," he said hopefully, but the lady shook her head.

"You must accept your defeat, Mr. Blythe, for I've won fair and square. And I only wish we'd set a very high stake before we began playing."

"Never mind, I'll pay for your dinner," he declared handsomely.

She gave him a saucy smile. "You would have done anyway—I'm your wife, remember?"

It was much colder now than when they had started the journey, and at the next posting-house they descended from the chaise to await the change of horses indoors. Nerissa drank a cup of tea by the fireplace and Nick stood at the window, warming his insides with brandy, when he saw their postboy stump out of the stable on his short bowed legs, his creased face set in ominous lines. Excusing himself, Nick went out to consult with the man.

"Is there a problem?" she asked when he rejoined her.

"With the harness," he replied. "One of the metal links has snapped—the one that holds the breeching strap to the collar. But happily there's an ironmonger in the village, and the postboy has gone to fetch him. We may as well dine here, for I should think it will be some time before the repair is completed."

He was amused when his companion vented her frustration by kicking out at the fender like an impatient child. "Oh, of *all* the misfortunes!" she cried. "I've never undertaken a journey so fraught with difficulties at every turn!"

"If you consider this a difficult journey, then you haven't travelled very much," said Nick, and after delivering this friendly scold, he went to order their dinner.

That night, much later than either of them expected, the weary travellers reached the Staffordshire town of Leek. Nerissa accepted the fact that she would have to put up at an inn for the night; it was a most unsuitable hour for descending upon even the closest of friends. As she told Nick Blythe, a household with three young children would have retired many hours ago, and he agreed that it was very likely.

"If only that stupid man hadn't taken so long with the harness," she fumed. "What a miserable little village that was! We never did learn the name of it, did we? So much time lost—but I suppose it's useless to cavil over that now."

"It is," Nick agreed.

She sighed. "Just as well that I don't go to Laura's house, for I'm no fit company after such a day as we've had." Looking over at him, she smiled and said, "You are very patient with me, Mr. Blythe. Forgive me for being so tiresome."

"I expect a glass of wine, a warm fire, and a good night's rest will set you to rights." He reached for her hand, saying, "Only think how far we have travelled together in these twenty-four hours, a journey I will always measure in friendship more than mere miles."

The carriage began to slow down. Nerissa was saddened to think that soon they would part and go their separate ways, never to meet again. She would be safe and secure in the midst of a loving family, while he journeyed on alone towards the port at Holyhead. His crossing to Ireland might be a treacherous one; the autumn gales in the Irish Channel were notoriously fierce. And when he did reach the opposite shore, he would enter into a lonely, solitary exile. Whatever his crime, he did not deserve so dismal a fate.

During the course of the long day, she had come to loathe the sight of any roadside establishment, but the George at Leek was far pleasanter than many they'd visited. A plump, efficient landlady conducted her to an upstairs room and made her perfectly comfortable there. A little while later, a maidservant delivered a verbal message from Mr. Blythe, who invited her to join him in his private parlour. Nerissa declined, pleading weariness, a convenient excuse as well as being a true one. Now that she'd resumed the style of a single lady, she was reluctant to arouse comment by doing anything unusual—she had learned that lesson all too well. But she spent the hour or so before going to bed regretting her decision, and hoping he hadn't felt slighted by her refusal.

The next morning she took pains with her toilette, for although she knew Laura would rejoice to see her even if her clothes were undistinguished and her coiffure less than fashionable, she well remembered her friend's elegance. While she washed and dressed, she was aware of the bustle of the inn. Doors opened and closed, and she could hear the frantic footsteps of the servants in the passage and the stamping of hooves beneath her window. It seemed that everyone was departing all at once.

Fearful that Nick Blythe might be of their number, she speedily finished her preparations and hurried downstairs. She found him in a small private parlour, reading a newspaper. At her entrance he laid it aside and came forward to greet her, looking much as he had when she'd first met him—deeply troubled.

"Good morning, Miss Newby," he said gravely. "I was on the point of sending a message to you."

Had he planned to depart without bidding her a personal farewell, after all she'd done for him? "I came down to—to say good-bye," she faltered, "before you leave."

"I will certainly not do so before I've broken my fast. And definitely not until I've seen you safely settled with your friends."

Vastly relieved, Nerissa sat down in the chair he pulled out for her. Soon a waiter brought them hot rolls and steaming coffee, and she readily partook of both. Mr. Blythe picked up his paper, and Nerissa knew better than to disturb him; her father had been no fit companion until he had gleaned every scrap of war news from his favourite journal. She didn't mind his abstraction, which permitted her to observe him closely without his being aware. The dark coat looked all the better for a good brushing, and his ebony locks had been coaxed into neat waves. He looked every inch the gentleman, and she would not be the least bit ashamed to introduce him to the Sedgewicks.

When he folded up his newspaper, his face was still grim, and she asked if he had been reading the war dispatches. "No," he replied, "it was the London news that caught my eye." From the way he had said this, she surmised that it hadn't pleased him very much.

They received directions to Mr. Sedgewick's house from their waiter, and within an hour they set out. After passing a spacious marketplace, they turned down a broad street banked by uniform brick houses and stopped at one situated midway down the row. Mr. Blythe beat a tattoo with the brass knocker, and he smiled at her as they waited.

An enormously fat woman opened the door to them. Her scowling face was composed of bulges of flesh in the place of cheeks, chin, mouth, and jowls. "What is it?" she asked, in less than welcoming accents.

"I am Miss Newby," Nerissa announced. "Mrs. Sedgewick is expecting me."

The woman's expression became more hostile. "Are you sure?" When Nerissa nodded, she heaved an exasperated, alcohol-flavoured sigh. "Oh, very well, I suppose you'd best come in, then, but the mistress made no mention of visitors to *me!*" This omission was clearly a sore point.

Nerissa cast an uncertain glance at Mr. Blythe before accepting the woman's curt invitation.

The house was deathly silent. Where, she wondered, was the happy laughter of the children, and the scampering of their small feet up and down the stairs? And search though she might, she could find nothing of Laura's quiet dignity in the decoration of the drawing-room to which she and the gentleman were led—and where they were abandoned. The burgundy damask that covered the walls and the chairs was too dark, and the arrangement of the several pictures was neither artful nor pleasing. She had a wealth of time to ponder these inconsistencies before another female arrived on the scene.

This one was as angular as the other had been rotund, and her voice was a near-whisper when she said, "You wished to see me?"

Nerissa, now completely bewildered, barely refrained from staring. "There must be some mistake— I asked for Mrs. Sedgewick. I wrote to tell her I was coming here."

"I *am* Mrs. Sedgewick, and I've had no letters this week. Who are you?"

A swift glance at Mr. Blythe's impassive face bolstered Nerissa's courage. "I am so sorry, we must have intruded upon you in error. Foolish of me not to guess there might be more than one Sedgewick family in Stockwell Street! Can you tell me if Mr. Henry Sedgewick, the lawyer, is one of your neighbours? The lady I am seeking is his wife."

All of a sudden the woman's bony face was transformed into a mask of fury. "You have indeed come here in error if you expected to find *that* hussy under my roof!" she declared with considerable heat. "Who are you? One of madam's fancy London friends, I'll be bound." Her pale eyes darted towards the gentleman, and she spat, "It's just like that wretched Laura to run off without informing me that she was expecting company!"

"Do you mean to say that she does live here?" Nerissa asked.

"Not for a fortnight past," was the venomous reply. "She's gone now. With her abigail, the children, Nurse—*and* my Henry. My only, my dearest boy! She lured him away, the spiteful thing, from the very mother that bore him!"

When Mrs. Sedgewick, senior, dropped into a chair and gave way to sobs, Nerissa's only desire was to beat a hasty retreat. She waited for the woman's moans to subside before saying, "I regret causing you any further distress, ma'am, but could you possibly tell me where Laura went?"

"I don't know, nor do I care! My Henry had no reason to leave Leek—he had respectable clients, his business here was prospering. But she took it into her head that he could do better for himself—in London, I daresay. I don't know what she said to convince him, and I can only guess how she must have maligned me. To be sure," Mrs. Sedgewick said bitterly, *"some* people consider her a beauty, but I never saw it myself. My servants didn't suit her fine notions, and when Henry accused poor Mrs. Grant of cheating me in the household accounts she took his part, the sly thing. Spent too much time in the nursery, too, and so I told her, again and again."

"Perhaps, but—"

"And my poor Henry, to be taken in by those quiet ways of hers. Well, still waters run deep, and I don't doubt she's been hatching her plot to wrest him away from me since the moment he slipped the ring on her finger. She was always jealous of me!"

Nerissa did not doubt that Mr. Sedgewick had voluntarily moved his family to London, for no son, however loving, could be expected to live comfortably with a mother like this. Her long-held vision of the Sedgewick's domestic bliss was shattered, and she wondered how Laura could have shared a home with such an ill-tempered woman and yet give no hint of any household strife in her letters.

She was exceedingly grateful to Mr. Blythe for stepping forward to extricate her from this hopeless situation. "We will be putting up at the George for the present," he told the weeping lady. "If you should receive any communication from your son—or his wife—within the next day or so, Miss Newby would like to be informed of their direction."

Mrs. Sedgewick's only response was to hide her face in her handkerchief.

A few minutes later, dazed and despondent, Nerissa found herself standing in the middle of Stockwell Street. "I can't begin to think what I'm supposed to do with myself now," she said.

It was, she realised, the first time she had admitted defeat. Throughout her father's illness and after his death, she had found the strength to go on, knowing he would expect her to be brave. Somehow she had survived the ordeal of being the favourite subject of gossip in Olney, and she'd had the courage to break her engagement to Andrew Hudgins. And throughout the strange events of the past two days she had displayed what she considered to be a remarkable degree of fortitude. But all along she'd been sustained by hope and the certainty that at the end of the road she would find a respite from the troubles that had plagued her of late. Now it turned out that the safe, happy refuge she had sought did not exist, and her one friend was lost to her.

Turning to her only possible source of consolation and comfort, she confessed, "I've never felt so completely alone in all my life."

"You didn't fail me in my hour of need," the gentleman reminded her. "Don't despair, my dear, for

you are not without a friend. Did no one ever tell you
that good deeds sometimes come home to roost?''

When he held out his arm to her, she placed her
trembling hand upon it, and let him lead her down the
street.

5

WHEN THEY RETURNED to the George, Nick parted from Nerissa in the vestibule, with the promise that they would meet again at dinner. She nodded absently, gave him a lopsided smile, and made her graceful way towards the staircase. As soon as he heard the faint opening and closing of her chamber door, he left the inn.

The skies were ominously grey and the wind on the rise. He walked aimlessly along the busy streets populated by strangers, occasionally pausing to look into a shop window. The parish church, Leek's most notable landmark, crowned a piece of high ground, and he strolled in that direction. He climbed to the summit, from which vantage point he was able to count the brick smokestacks belonging to the various local manufactories, a grim contrast to the gentle hills beyond the town. For some minutes he gazed upon the miniature world spread out before him, marvelling that its ceaseless rhythm was unaltered and quite unaffected by the small tragedies in the lives of the individuals inhabiting it.

The churchyard was graced by a sandstone monument, a pyramid engraved with curious images. After a brief, disinterested examination, Nick sat down upon its base and leaned his back against the solid surface. The wind was merciless, but he hardly felt it; the constant, dull ache in his heart effectively blotted out the sensation.

His perusal of the *London Gazette* had made it painfully clear that he was still an object of notoriety. Column after column had been chock-full of details—all false—of his purported *affaire* with Lady Titus. Public outcry against duelling was great, according to the paper, and he guessed that the less reputable printers of Grub Street were producing sensational and incendiary pamphlets, which would destroy any chance of a fair trial, should it ever come to that. All along, in the back of his mind, he had believed he could return to London at any time and clear his name of the murder charge. Recalling the disturbing accounts he'd read thus far, he knew that to make an attempt now would be sheer folly. Perhaps someday—but perhaps never, and it was better to accept what there was no changing.

At least, he thought, trying to cheer himself, his possessions were protected. For the remainder of his life, no other person could lay claim to his title and fortune. However long he must remain in exile, his lawyers would continue to act on his behalf, and his steward, a trustworthy man, was well qualified to manage his Wiltshire estate. Moreover, because the property was not entailed, none of his family—and here he thought of his cousin Ramsey, who most needed the money—could profit from having him declared legally dead in the future. But in the event of his untimely demise, everything he owned would go to his nearest male relative, as specified in the only will he had ever made. It had been drawn up long ago, when his only assets had been his horses and his books and the legacy his mother had left him, and it had not been updated at the time of his father's death. There was no way to prevent his title from devolving upon Ramsey. But the thought of his cousin selfishly squan-

dering the substantial Blythe rents on hunters and
hounds angered him beyond reason. He'd always intended to name Justin the heir to his real property but
had never quite got around to doing anything; this
oversight tortured him, helpless as he was to remedy
it.

Lifting his head, he stared out at the panorama of
town and country intently, as if it held some answer
to the questions tumbling about in his mind. The longer he looked, the more reluctant he was to leave England for Ireland, that alien land. And why should he?
This journey from hamlet to village to marketplace
had reminded him of that vast world beyond London,
and as he gazed upon the distant hills, he wondered if
hiding himself in some remote, rural corner of England would be preferable to seeking refuge across the
channel. He had already created a new identity, and
as Nick Blythe, Esquire, he ought to be able to build
a whole new life for himself.

And who better to share it with him, he thought,
smiling, than that lovely, lost creature back at the
inn, who by her own admission had no home, no
friends, and no relations to speak of?

He could not marry her, of course. Despite her many
and manifold charms, he had no desire to be irrevo-
cably bound to her. His family was a respected one;
his pride in that ancient name and lineage would not
permit him to take just any female to wife. Nerissa
Newby was beautiful and well mannered, and she possessed a striking intellect, but he required something
more in the way of pedigree. If she was indeed a prod-
uct of the merchant class, which seemed to be the
case, that in itself would be no real impediment to a
union. But there was also the fact that she had borne
a bastard child, and the future Lady Blythe could not
carry so indelible a stain into matrimony. Someday his
need for an heir would compel him to take a wife, for

a son would be an undisputed claimant to his title and lands. That being so, it was unfortunate that his scruples prevented him from marrying Miss Newby, who was, if nothing else, a proven breeder.

That evening he dressed for dinner with as much care as if he were about to tender a genuine offer of matrimony. Before putting on one of the new shirts Cat had procured for him in St. Albans, he washed himself, energetically splashing soap and water from the basin, his mind still busy fashioning arguments that might induce Miss Newby to throw her lot in with his. If she had thought him mad when he begged her to shelter him in Lutterworth, he could just imagine how she would react to his proposal that they live together without benefit of clergy. She might not regard him as any great bargain, but certainly she was in no position to pick and choose when it came to protectors.

He elected to wear his kerseymere breeches rather than the travel-worn buckskins he had been sporting for so many days. After arranging the folds of his cravat with precision, he fastened it with a gold pin, a gift from his father. Surveying himself in a looking-glass smoky with age, he wondered if Miss Newby would be inclined to look upon him with favour.

When she joined him in his private parlour at the appointed hour, he saw that she, too, had taken some pains with her appearance. She wore a cambric gown the colour of fine burgundy, with a low, square neckline and long sleeves. He led her over to the table, its snowy cloth nearly obscured by an array of dishes and utensils, and told her, "I ordered several courses, and the first of them should arrive at any moment. Although I have much to say to you, I would prefer to wait in order that we may avoid any interruption."

She nodded her assent, and took her seat.

As he filled her glass with wine, he asked pleasantly, "How did you pass the afternoon?"

"Idly, I'm afraid. I kept to my bedchamber—with a young rogue named Tom Jones as my companion," she added with an impish smile.

"And did he entertain you well?"

"Certainly he put me in a rather more cheerful mood than my circumstances would seem to warrant." Nerissa picked up her napkin and placed it in her lap. "It's my misfortune that whoever occupied my room before me left behind only the first volume of Fielding's novel."

"You are fond of reading?" Nick asked.

"Very. I had free run of Papa's library from an early age. He always said that if I was able to reach a book, then I was old enough to be permitted to read it. So my Aunt Portia made sure to keep the most titillating forms of literature on the topmost shelf, and she placed all her housekeeping and cookery books well within my grasp!"

The waiter entered the room at that moment, and their conversation suffered his intrusion. The first course that was laid before them included a roast chicken smothered in wine sauce, a raised pie, and a hasty pudding. Nerissa sampled everything yet ate little, but Nick, as a result of the day's mental and physical exertions, applied himself to the task of polishing off his share of the meal. When the dishes were cleared away and the cloth removed, Nerissa took a few sugared almonds before retiring to the settee.

When Nick asked if she would mind if he smoked, the lady said promptly, "Not in the least. Papa always did so after dinner, and I quite like the smell of tobacco."

He selected a long-stemmed clay pipe from the case on the mantel and reached into his coat pocket for his tobacco pouch. He filled the bowl with the aromatic weed, tamped it down, then lit it with a spill. After summoning up all the persuasive speeches he had been memorising all afternoon, he sat down in an armless chair across from the sofa. "I've been trying to determine how I can best help you, Nerissa," he began.

"That must have been a singularly unrewarding pastime," she commented. "But you may be easy, Mr. Blythe, for I assure you that I don't depend upon you to help me."

"Perhaps not, but still I feel some responsibility towards you. I did place you in a position of danger—remember, I am yet a hunted man. The law is seeking me even as we sit here, cosy and safe in the wilds of Staffordshire."

"Laura Sedgewick's untimely absence from Leek is hardly your fault," she persisted. "I would have found myself at *point-non-plus* whether or not you had accompanied me to that house this morning. But you mustn't concern yourself—I daresay I shall simply go to London."

Nick drew thoughtfully on his pipe, wondering if she would seek out her former lover, the father of her child. "Do I perceive a certain reluctance to take that step?"

"I think we may deal in reality rather than perception, Mr. Blythe," she said crisply. "The facts of my situation are very, very clear. For reasons that I shall not go into, I managed to scandalise my village to the extent that I was obliged to leave it. My reputation is shattered, perhaps irreparably. My friend is out of reach. And though I do have a little money of my own, it hardly matters, for in every other respect I am quite destitute."

He was impressed by this speech, for she had managed to deliver it without investing a single syllable with self-pity. "People are so fond of saying that money can't purchase happiness," he mused, "but for a moment let's pretend that it could. I wonder what sort of life would most content you, Nerissa. Tell me, what would you ordain for yourself, if you were able?''

Softly she replied, ''I would want to live quietly, as I did in Olney. Although I should like to feel useful—I'd want some sense of purpose—I would require a reasonable measure of independence, for I've always had that. As for material things, well, I would be happy with a pleasant house and plenty of books, and perhaps a garden to work.''

The simplicity of her catalogue delighted Nick, for he instantly saw how he might use it to his advantage. ''But surely you would need a companion to share your Arcadia. I don't believe we humans are capable of being completely happy in solitude. Hermits are very rare, Nerissa.''

A shadow passed over her face. ''But no power in the world can restore my father to me. I am destined always to be alone, for no one can ever take his place in my life. Andrew Hudgins would have been a sorry substitute, and I was far from being the proper woman for him—he wanted perfection in a wife, something Papa never expected from his daughter. His tolerance may well have been responsible for my downfall, but I cannot regret it. My mistake was imputing a similar tolerance to others of my acquaintance.''

Nick supposed this was the most she would ever tell him about her disgrace, even though she hadn't mentioned her child directly. It was apparent to him that the broad-minded Captain Newby had accepted the result of his daughter's indiscretion, but her Mr. Hudgins had not. Now, bereft of father, fiance, and child, this brave, unbowed girl had left her home, intent upon making a fresh start, only to be thwarted at the outset.

''What is your age, Nerissa?'' he asked her.

''Twenty-three.''

''You are at once too young and yet too old to find

yourself so alone in the world.'' He lifted the pipe to his lips and inhaled deeply, expelling the smoke in rings. He watched them dissipate, then said, ''You say you seek some peaceful retreat, but I fear you will never find it in London. I have lived there, and I know. Nor can you, as impulsive and strong-minded as you are, ever be happy living a highly restricted life with some paid companion to lend you a false respectability.'' He abandoned his chair, and after taking a turn about the room he told her abruptly, ''I have changed my mind about going to Ireland. There will be a watch on at Holyhead port, and the constabulary on the other side of the channel may have been alerted by now.'' Remembering his determination to be frank, he gave her a slight smile and said ruefully, ''The fact of the matter is, I simply don't *wish* to leave England, any more than you want to go to London.''

Her fathomless blue eyes stared back at him. ''But what will you do?''

''I've decided to continue travelling north, as far as the Scottish border. I've funds enough to set up as a gentleman farmer in some remote area where no one can connect me with my crime. And,'' he concluded, his heart already pounding in anticipation of her reply, ''I want you to go with me.''

For the space of several seconds, she hardly seemed to breathe. Finally, after a startled intake of air she echoed faintly, ''Go with you? In—in what capacity?''

''As my companion in adversity.''

He was encouraged by the smile that played at the corners of her generous mouth. ''That is certainly a vague reply,'' she said.

''I'm asking you to live with me,'' he elaborated. ''I cannot hold out false promises merely to soothe your sensibilities, so I tell you quite frankly that ours would be a sham marriage. But in the eyes of the world you would be my wife, and for the sake of convention,

I would expect you to take my name." He read the shock in her face and strove for a soothing note when he said, "I don't demand an immediate answer. You must take the time to consider very carefully, for I am content to wait, if I improve my chances by so doing." Satisfied that he had been as forthright as he vowed to be, he walked over to the fireplace to empty the ash from his pipe and deposited it on the mantelshelf.

While his back was turned he heard her say, "Mr. Blythe, I want to be quite sure that I understand the terms of this—this partnership you are proposing. You offer me your protection and your name, in return for which I am to keep your house and cook your meals?"

Nick shook his head. "No, no, I certainly don't demand that you become a household drudge! You will be the wife of a gentleman, we will have servants—as many as you like. If you want to raise hens or dirty your hands in the rosebeds, it will be your decision, not by my command."

"But we hardly know each other."

"Time will soon remedy that." Despite this assurance, she frowned slightly, so he said, "Do not mistrust my motives; for I don't think I've ever given you cause to do so. I don't require that you become my mistress, Nerissa."

Privately, however, he had his hopes. From the very beginning of their association he had been conscious of her opulent beauty, and tonight her lavish figure was revealed to his eyes as never before. She might be wary of him now, but she was no virginal miss. She had already sampled the pleasures of love, and he could not doubt that she had found them to her liking. He would not force her to his bed, but neither did he believe it would remain empty for very long. But more than anything he wanted her to feel comfortable with him, and in order to settle any lingering concerns he added, "I seek your friendship and your companionship, Nerissa. In whatever fashion they come to me, I will be satisfied."

She did not answer immediately. Finally she said, "I appreciate your candour, for I value it above anything. Except tolerance," she amended.

"I am tolerant, too," he said silkily, "and generous. And patient and kind and anything else you most admire in men." The sudden blaze of reproach in her eyes chastened him, and he said, "Forgive me, I know you won't be won over by tricks and stratagems. Nor will I try to convince you with unceasing argument. If you cannot come with me willingly, then it is best you do not come at all."

The lady's thick, dark lashes swept downward. After a brief study of the carpet, she looked up and said, "I promise I will think on all you've said—I daresay I shall think of nothing else. But for now, if you will be so good as to excuse me, I would like to return to my room."

Just as she reached the door, he stopped her, saying, "Before you go, Nerissa, will you answer me one question?" She signalled her willingness by facing him, but her expression was wary. "If I offered to make you my wife, legally and by church rite, would you accept me more readily?"

"No," she said, "I don't think I would. I'm not sure that a true marriage of convenience is preferable to a pretend one, Mr. Blythe. In some ways, I think it might even be worse."

She left him, and as he watched her go, Nick warned himself that he would be wise to prepare for a disappointment.

For the third night in a row, Nerissa could hardly sleep for thinking about Nick Blythe, tossing and turning in yet another unfamiliar bed in yet another strange inn. Despite her uncertainty, one thing was apparent to her: she could do whatever she pleased, for there was not a soul alive who cared where she went, or with whom.

Her de Tourzel relations were simply too far away to be of any use to her, nor was Jersey a suitable or a safe haven for a solitary young woman—or anyone else, these days. When Uncle Claude had written to her after her father's death, he had described the island as a place where the people lived in constant fear of French invasion. The peace of St. Helier, the principal town, was forever disturbed by the brawling pirates and privateers who had made the port their headquarters. The de Tourzels were well off, they owned farmland and town property, but they were strangers to Nerissa. No doubt they would welcome a visit from Gabrielle's only child, but would any of them be willing to provide her with a permanent home?

On her paternal side, her prospects were only slightly better. Her papa's first cousin, the Duke of Solway, had four grown children of his own, and he was guardian to his fatherless niece and nephew. Besides, he and his duchess moved in the highest circles of society, and Nerissa would be woefully out of place in their exalted world. She had made a few, brief visits to the duke's country seat during her youth, and he had been a frequent visitor to the house in the Adelphi Terrace. But upon leaving Olney she had been reluctant to seek His Grace's protection, and after several days of travelling through England's heartland with a notorious duellist, she was even less eager to do so. There would be no covering up the unhappy fact that she was doubly ruined now.

She did not doubt that if she were deathly ill or in grave danger, her relations would come to her aid. But she was not in such dire straits as that; her problem was simply that she didn't know what to do with herself. Her trustees, a banker and a lawyer, were busy men, far more interested in her assets than her personal welfare. Mr. Halpern and Mr. Rose spoke the language of Funds and Consols and shares and capital, and not once since her papa's death had either of them asked if she was unhappy, or lonely—or bored. In their eyes she was simply a collection of documents in a black tin box with the Newby name painted on the lid.

She could acquit Mr. Blythe of coveting her fortune, because he did not know she was an heiress. And he had not asked her to do anything that she had not already done; she had passed herself off as his bride during their first night together, in Lutterworth, and for the whole of the following day. Being a fugitive, he would want to live very retired—something that appealed to a young woman who was weary of being stared at and gossiped about. He held out the promise of the sort of life she had known at her father's side, and that was a strong inducement indeed.

It was not even an alien notion to her, that a couple should share a home without being married. As a child she had known the poet Mr. Cowper and his devoted friend Mrs. Unwin, the widow who had kept house for him. They had lived together in unwedded bliss for some three decades, and despite the irregularity of their liaison, Nerissa's aunt and everyone else in the neighbourhood had received them.

But Nick Blythe would be bound to make advances, sooner or later, no matter what he'd said to the contrary, for he couldn't be completely impervious to the quality in her that had attracted so many others before him. This troubled her, but she knew her powers of resistance, and besides, he could easily find some other female to supply the kind of companionship she was unwilling to provide him.

Try as she might, she was unable to churn up any strenuous objections to his scheme. The odd thing was, she had no real reason not to accept Nick Blythe's offer, and ironically, that was why she found it so difficult to do so.

In the morning she faced the looking-glass with trepidation. As she had feared, she wore her woes in her face, and soap and water went only a little way towards lessening the ravages of another sleepless night. To her own critical eyes she looked infinitely older, and without the advantage of feeling any wiser. When she went down to breakfast, she still did not know how she would answer Mr. Blythe's inevitable question. She entered the parlour with a skipping pulse, but when she took her place at the table he did nothing more alarming than wish her good morning, adding that it was the day of the village fair. This was unexpected, so far removed from the thundering "Well?" for which she was still so miserably unprepared, that she had trouble thinking of a reply.

"Should you like to go with me?"

"To the fair?" she asked, fearing that he had suddenly and unceremoniously reverted to the subject that had kept her awake for so many hours.

"I thought we might disport ourselves among the locals, for it would be a shame to waste such a day as this." He gestured towards the window with his knife.

Where, she wondered, was the lust-driven ogre that had figured in her worst imaginings during the long night? The man who obligingly passed her the butter was the same polite, handsome gentleman she had known for the past—why, could this really be the fourth day of their acquaintance? Surely an eternity had passed since the afternoon their paths had crossed in the inn yard at Northampton.

Meeting his eyes, clear and grey, she smiled. "Yes, I would." And then, lest he had mistaken her answer as she had his question, she elaborated, "I'd like to go to the fair. Very much."

Later, when they joined the country-folk who had

converged upon Leek, Nerissa could almost believe
her escort had forgotten their conversation of the night
before. But while she followed him from stall to stall
and pretended to admire the cabbages and parsnips on
display, she was still wrestling with the question of
whether or not she ought to accept his offer.

She was so much distracted that she failed to notice
that they had become separated. As soon as she did
realise he had left her side, she was seized by the fear
that he had deliberately abandoned her. The cries of
the hawkers and the roar of the multitude rang in her
ears, intensifying her panic, and she was continually
jostled by the press of bodies all around her. After
fighting her way to a market stall, she rose on tiptoe
to scan the crowd with anxious eyes, but Nick Blythe
was nowhere to be seen. An apple-woman began a
long-winded harangue, praising her wares, and since
Nerissa had no intention of buying, she had to move
on. A Punch and Judy show loomed ahead of her, so
she joined the group of children and adults that clus-
tered around the booth. They shouted with laughter at
the puppet play, but Nerissa could barely muster a
smile, not even when the argumentative Punch took
up his cudgel and flailed everything in sight.

Although she saw the appreciative leer on the face
of the burly man standing next to her, she ignored
him. When he began to sidle up to her, she pretended
not to notice, but this cavalier reception of his attentions emboldened him to fling his arm about her waist.
"Come with me, pretty one," he drawled, his hot
breath searing her cheek, "and I'll buy you a fairing."

"Let me be, damn you!" she cried.

"Mind your language, wench, we mustn't shock the
wee ones." A ripple of laughter greeted his words;
some of the audience had turned to see what was going
on at the rear. When she tried to escape his impris-

oning hold, her grinning admirer gave her an admonitory pinch.

Nerissa stopped struggling. "Good sir," she said sweetly, *"Here's* a fairing to remember *me* by." He leaned forward expectantly, and she dealt his red, sweaty face a resounding blow with her open palm. There was a burst of applause from the onlookers, and the man walked off, muttering curses and rubbing his cheek.

"Well done," said a familiar, husky voice from behind.

Nerissa whirled around to find Nick Blythe smiling down at her. "There you are," she breathed in relief.

"I'm happy that you chose to decline his invitation—it would be quite lowering to lose you to such a rival as that."

She tossed her head. "Fie, sir, I'm never the sort to run off with just any man who asks."

"No, of course not," he agreed, but his eyes were gently mocking. "Naturally you are very selective, or you would not be in my company now. Come along, minx, before you get into trouble again. There's a sight you cannot miss—the most famous juggler in all Christendom!" He took her by the hand and led her to a nearby platform where a man in a tunic and particoloured hose was tossing apples. Although a placard described him as a favourite at every court in Europe, the sadly bruised fruit bore testimony to his lack of skill—and veracity.

After watching him bend down again and again to retrieve his apples, Nerissa and Nick, their sides aching with laughter, finally abandoned the fair. They found a pleasant, tree-lined footpath that led away from the village, and followed it, neither much caring where it might take them. The afternoon was typical of October, sunny and clear, but a faint chill in the air was a reminder that this month of abundant harvest was also a time of preparation for the grimmer season to come. As they walked along, Nerissa, locked in that continuing battle with her conflicting desires, kept her eyes fixed upon the colourful, haphazard patchwork of fallen leaves.

Something occurred to her, and she came to a sudden stop. "If I agree to go north, to live with you in obscurity, could I not pretend to be your sister?"

"I'm afraid you don't look very much like a sister," Nick said bluntly.

His reply wounded her a little, but she knew exactly what he meant by it. "I suppose not," she sighed.

"I would be honoured to acknowledge you as my kinswoman," he said when they walked on, "but you are intelligent enough to understand why that might arouse suspicion. If we are to live the sort of anonymous life I envision, you will have to put your mother's wedding ring back on your finger."

He was right, of course. Keeping her voice light, as though her question were merely a hypothetical one, she asked what would happen if they discovered that they weren't compatible.

"We can always dissolve our partnership and go our separate ways," he replied. "If someday you decide that you prefer to go to London, I can easily move on to some other remote locale and begin anew."

She was surprised that he made no further attempt to persuade her; surely he must see how close she was to capitulation. But he had, she recalled, told her that her decision must be a voluntary one, and clearly he was a man of his word.

Their stroll ended abruptly at the edge of a river, and so did Nerissa's arguments with herself. "I will go with you," she said, and when she turned to look at him, she caught the flash of triumph in his eyes. It was gone so quickly that she decided she must have imagined it, for surely he couldn't care so very much whether she accepted or refused him.

"You are quite sure?" he asked.

"I hate to think what my fate would be if I went to London. I prefer to take my chances with you, Mr. Blythe. What is the best method for sealing a bargain such as ours?"

"This, I think," Nick said, extending his hand, and his fingers closed over hers, even as his eyes strayed to her mouth. "Unless," he added daringly, "you regard a handshake as too formal and unfeeling."

Nerissa looked up at him curiously, never guessing he might accept it as an invitation to him to do what he did. The kiss lasted for the space of a heartbeat, but it was quite long enough to warn her, too late, that she was condemned to build her new life upon the very brink of temptation.

=== 6 ===

WHEN IN LONDON, Ramsey Blythe lived in a set of rooms in Carrington Street, a convenient situation for a man of his tastes, being but a short walk from the sacred precincts of Tattersall's Repository. He seldom missed a sale-day, and one Monday morning in the middle of October he could be found standing in the shade of the graceful colonnade, watching the progress of a handsome bay gelding that was being paraded around the enclosure.

He had often stood in that same spot with his father, a gambler and an avid huntsman, who had all but beggared himself pursuing his ruinously expensive hobbies. The family coffers had been too empty to permit an Oxford education; Ramsey had received his schooling on the hunting field and at the gaming tables. Viscount Cavender, after raising his eldest son in his own image, had broken his neck in a fall from his horse, and at eighteen Ramsey found himself responsible for his father's massive debts, his widowed mother, and his young brother Justin. Lady Cavender had long practised stringent household economies in a futile attempt to make up for her husband's excesses, but the extent of his obligations was such that Ramsey wondered why she had bothered. Knowing he could never hope to keep it up, he had offered to sell the freehold of the London house to Baron Blythe, his paternal uncle, nearest neighbour, and sole trustee. The imposing mansion in Grosvenor Square, duly renamed Blythe House, passed to the other branch of the family, and the purchase price permitted Ramsey to settle with the most pressing of his father's creditors.

Shortly after attaining his majority, he made up his mind to seek a tenant for Cavender Chase. The thought of strangers living there was abhorrent to him, but he needed more money than the encumbered estate could produce. His mother stoically agreed to vacate her home, but she had demanded one thing, that her younger son be allowed to continue at Eton. She made it clear that she would spend her own jointure, if necessary, to send Justin to Oxford and she was equally determined that one day he should read jurisprudence. Ramsey, no less eager to see his brother established in a profession that would ensure his self-sufficiency, promised to contribute what he could to Justin's education. Satisfied, Lady Cavender went to live with Lord and Lady Blythe in that same London house she had once been mistress of, and Ramsey leased his ancestral home to a wealthy Cit at a very high rent.

He had just been able to afford a small string of hunters, and was thus able to follow his predecessor's example, spending the greater part of the year in the shires, riding to hounds, and the rest of it at boxing matches and prize fights and race meetings. And that October afternoon at Tattersall's, he found himself in the sort of company he most liked. He was one of a large group of men of all ages and every degree of fashion, which included courtiers and commoners, grooms, stableboys, kennel-masters, coachmen, jockeys, and horse-dealers. And as his brown eyes scanned the crowd, he could count numerous friends and acquaintances. Feeling the need of some refreshment, he went to the spacious taproom, and there fell in with a party of younger men who solicited his opinion on the bay gelding, and a fine chestnut filly that had been on show earlier in the day.

"We missed you at Melton a fortnight ago," said one fellow, the scion of a noble house.

Ramsey shrugged diffidently, but a flush stained his tanned countenance as he recalled the reason for his absence. He had lost a great deal of money at the August Meeting at York, when he had backed Allegro, ridden by the famed Newmarket jockey, Mr. Buckle, against the filly Louisa, ridden by a noted equestrienne, the wife of Colonel Thornton. The lady rider had won the race, and to cover his bets Ramsey had sold off three of his best hunters. And although he admitted this fact to Lord Albert, he hoped his presence would encourage everyone to think he'd come to Tattersall's to replace his horses. He kept to himself the dismal truth, that he lacked the funds—or the credit—to purchase any of the handsome animals being shown, or the meanest of the many phaetons and curricles for sale.

"Bought one of your cast-offs myself," one gentleman declared, "that long-tailed grey you was always so proud of—Samson. Carried me on a capital run our last day at Melton—can't imagine why you didn't keep him. What stamina the poor brute had," he said, shaking his head sorrowfully.

"Had?" Ramsey choked.

"My groom was exercising him t'other day, and the beast broke his knees taking a five-barred gate. I had to shoot him on the spot—the horse, not the groom, though I vow I was sore tempted!"

He fought to conceal his chagrin and disgust. The most beloved of all his mounts was now rotting in some ditch—or had he received that mark of distinction reserved for faithful hunters, and been fed to the hounds? Ramsey would not ask, nor could he, for his

friends had begun to talk of the duel, as nearly everyone seemed to be doing these days.

"I heard that his ladybird finally accepted *carte
blanche* from Tarrant," said the young lordling who
had remarked on Ramsey's absence from the Melton
hunt. "She must've given up hope that Blythe will return. Or else she's clever enough to know he'll have
scant use for her if he lands in Newgate!"

"Have a care, Bertie," someone cautioned him.

"What? Oh, sorry, Cavender. But it's no secret he
might have to stand trial for murder in the House of
Lords. Peers have been tried before, and have even
gone to the gallows. Think of Lord Ferrers," Lord
Albert added darkly.

"That was nearly fifty years ago," protested the man
who had bought and destroyed Samson. "I can't believe Nick Blythe killed a man in cold blood. Some
say the duel was forced upon him—Sir Algernon had
a damnably short temper, and a history of settling
grievances at pistol-point. And that jade he took as a
wife was flirting with half a dozen fellows I can name,
before and after the wedding."

"Well, if she had a lover, it couldn't have been
Blythe," Lord Albert pointed out. "He was perfectly
content with his doxy, the little Ellen. Ain't that so,
Cavender?"

"I—I believe he was," Ramsey faltered. His throat
suddenly felt dry, and he lifted his tankard. Ever since
that infamous duel, he'd fallen prey to the curious,
who, like Lord Albert, were eager to question him.
Day after day he'd read the newspaper accounts of his
cousin's alleged infamy, for the London printers had
sunk their teeth into the juiciest scandal to come their
way in years, and as yet had not grown sated. Reluctant to join in the speculation about where the Baron
had run to, Ramsey mumbled an excuse about an ap-

pointment with his tailor and made his escape from the taproom.

His cousin's duel had quite cut up his peace, for the whole world was buzzing about Lord Blythe and Lady Titus and poor, dead Sir Algernon. Ramsey wasn't much concerned that he could be connected with the recent unhappy events, for he'd been careful to keep his *affaire* with Georgiana a secret, and she wouldn't care to make it known, certainly not now. But perhaps he would be wise to call in Clifford Street, ostensibly to offer his condolences, just to make certain that her husband hadn't uttered some incriminating deathbed confession.

A domed temple housing a life-sized statue of Reynard stood in the courtyard, and as Ramsey passed it he heard a gruff voice exclaim, "By God, the very man I've been looking for this half hour!" He turned slowly, steeling himself for another encounter with one more person eager to talk of his cousin. But the man who accosted him was none other than his Uncle Isaac, who was accompanied by an impassive, black-eyed Indian manservant.

It was at Newmarket that Lord Cavender had first met the black sheep of the family. Mr. Isaac Meriden, after amassing a sizeable fortune during his two-score years in India, had returned to his native shores with the intention of purchasing a property in Leicestershire, where he would be close to his favourite hunts. When Ramsey had learned that his uncle required a female relation to keep house for him, he was quick to suggest his mother, and the long-suffering Lady Cavender left Blythe House and went to live with her brother.

"Good day to you, sir," he said, shaking hands. "I had no notion you were in town. Does my mother accompany you?" The old gentleman shook his head, to Ramsey's great relief. He was not close to his widowed parent, and supposed it was because he reminded her so much of his father. "Did you see that bay gelding?" he asked.

"Too rich for your blood, m'boy," Mr. Meriden said severely. "And it's a pity, he'd carry you well. Or me, only I'm not in the market for a hunter—came to Tatt's for a neat little mare, one that will be gentle in harness. I found her, too, and now I must buy a dog-cart. I thought your mother might enjoy tooling herself around the country." Ramsey dutifully enquired about his mother's health, and received a favourable account. "She's very well, very well indeed," the nabob said cheerfully. "It's lucky I met you here—saves me the trouble of calling in Carrington Street. I wish to discuss a business matter with you, provided you are at leisure this evening."

"I am."

"Then join me at Boodle's—eight o'clock. We'll dine together. This afternoon I'm meeting with my solicitor, and afterwards I must go to Lincoln's Inn and see if I can run young Justin to the ground; your mother has messages for him that I must deliver in person." The old gentleman frowned. "Lately his letters have been very full of Damon Lovell—I trust he ain't been getting into trouble now that the wild young marquis has taken him up?"

"Not that I know of," Ramsey answered.

"Glad to hear it. One scandal in the family is quite enough," said Mr. Meriden sternly.

That night Ramsey arrayed himself in his evening togs and presented himself at Boodle's in St. James in obedience to his uncle's wishes. He was not himself a club man, his meagre income did not provide the same luxuries that his fellow peers took for granted, but he spied several acquaintances as a footman led him to the coffee room where Mr. Meriden awaited him.

He did not look forward to this interview; he preferred any one of his sporting cronies to the whole pack of his relations—except for Justin, the only person who looked up to him. Ramsey, who believed that he was similarly devoted to his brother, never quite realised that his affection was more selfish than selfless. For a time Dominic Blythe had supplanted him as his brother's hero, and then at Oxford, Justin had met Damon Lovell, so much closer to him in age. Ramsey envied his cousins not only Justin's affection, but also their looks and their popularity with the fair sex—and their large fortunes.

The dinner was excellent, but he had to compete with the chops and puddings for his uncle's attention. After the covers were removed and a bottle of brandy placed on the table by one of the serving men, the conversation improved.

"How long will you be in town, Uncle?" Ramsey asked, after hearing a long, dull report about his mother's recent activities.

"I'm leaving tomorrow," Mr. Meriden announced. "After a week of putting up at Fladong's, I shall be glad to return to Leicestershire. My business is completed—or will be when I've talked it over with you. There's a meet at Swanborough Abbey at the week's end, and I don't want to miss it. D'you mean to attend?"

Ramsey shook his head regretfully, for the Swanborough pack and the country it hunted were renowned. "I've no longer got horses fit for that terrain, just a pair of cover-hacks."

Mr. Meriden narrowed his eyes. "A pity. You should've done as I did and gone to India to repair your fortunes, Ram. The place would suit you down to the ground. No one works terribly hard—too hot for that—and the society is lively. And there's a decent amount of sport to be had." He was silent for a few seconds, then said, "I came back from the East with more money than most men dream of, and as you know, I've no son to leave it to. Oh, I sired two bastards in Calcutta, and made provision for them before I left. Naturally I've never contemplated leaving my money to either of them, not when I've got a bevy of nephews, without even counting my second sister's brood. She refuses to receive me, so I feel no compunction to remember her or her brats in my will."

Ramsey began to listen more attentively.

"Sir Robert Meriden is a worthy fellow, but he's to be wed to one of Lord Rowan's girls next spring, which makes him ineligible."

"I believe my mother mentioned the engagement," Ramsey said diffidently. He couldn't imagine why his cousin's marriage should serve to put him out of the way of inheriting the nabob's fortune, but he couldn't be sorry for it.

"I must confess that at one time I considered making Celesta's son my heir," Mr. Meriden continued. "You won't remember her, but she was a sweet creature and always fond of me. But now I know young Damon rather better, I fear he's growing too much like his father—a cold, harsh man, who made my poor sister most unhappy. And the marquis needs none of my brass, for he's undoubtedly one of the wealthiest men of his generation."

That left only two other possibilities, and Ramsey's heart began to pound. It couldn't be Justin, he told himself, Justin was a younger son, he had a profession—or would have, when he completed his law studies.

"You, Ram, are the eldest of all my nephews, and although you are a Blythe, Meriden blood flows in your veins. You are yet unwed, which is something to the purpose, and you possess a title. So I have made up my mind to make you my heir."

Ramsey hardly knew what to say. His brain was reeling from the sudden and entirely unexpected news that one day he would be an extremely rich man. Striving for a sober note that would conceal his exultation, he replied, "Your generosity overwhelms me, sir."

Mr. Meriden shook his head. "I haven't finished. The inheritance would be conditional upon your accepting my terms. For I'm not only offering you a fortune, but a bride as well. If you want the one, you must agree to take the other. The young lady's birth is impeccable—she's the daughter of an earl and niece to a duke." Mr. Meriden's sallow face softened, and his voice was gentle when he said, "You needn't worry that she's lacking in beauty, or charm, for she has both. In abundance."

"I am all eagerness to make her acquaintance," Ramsey said. He didn't greatly care what the chit was like; he'd agree to wed a gorgon if he could enrich himself by so doing.

"For all I know, you may have met her already. You've hunted with the Swanborough pack, and she is the earl's only sister."

But Ramsey, an infrequent visitor to Swanborough Abbey, had no memory of any young lady there. Lord Swanborough was yet a child, and the ward of his uncle, the Duke of Solway. "I do believe I helped his lordship onto his pony once, but he is so young that I never thought he might have a sister of marriageable age."

"Lady Miranda Peverel is only seventeen," Mr. Meriden replied. "She and the little boy make their home with the Marchants." In a confidential tone he said, "It is not generally spoken of, but the birth of young Ninian was hard on his mother. The Countess of Swanborough is a complete invalid and lives in Bath in the constant care of a physician. She was the Lady Hermia Marchant, the duke's prettiest sister and my own sweetheart. I'd have married her, too, if I hadn't fallen into a scrape and been shipped off to India by my father.''

Ramsey, amused by his uncle's sentimental reason for promoting the match, stated his willingness to enter into an engagement. ''But, sir, this bud of perfection might prefer to choose her own husband. I believe girls of seventeen can have very definite notions about suitors. And I doubt that her guardian will welcome the addresses of a penniless peer so many years her senior.''

''Oh, Duke William and I are old friends,'' the nabob said airily. ''I will drop a word in his ear about your prospects. As for your age, there's nothing can be done about it, and anyway it's common knowledge that young ladies will often develop a *tendre* for an older gentleman. You're a hunting man, and she grew up among such—your horsemanship will win her, I'll be bound. And you are no longer penniless, far from it.'' Mr. Meriden reached into his coat pocket. ''Here's a draft on my bank. It should enable you to purchase as many hunters as you please. As soon as the banns are published, I'll undertake to provide you with an independence—then you can take up residence at Cavender Chase again. I can't let you house Lady Mira in your Carrington Street lodging, now can I?''

Ramsey, delighted by the vast sum scrawled upon the face of the cheque, thanked his uncle profusely. But he could not help saying, ''An allowance and a bride all in one day—you go much too fast for me, Uncle.''

''Not fast enough,'' his uncle contradicted him. ''It so happens that the lass is very friendly with her Marchant cousins. Both are well-looking young men, and the elder will be duke someday. Besides which, a multitude of other eligibles have descended upon Leicestershire this autumn, and as soon as word goes 'round that Solway's niece is an Incomparable, you'll be left in the dust.'' He rubbed his nose with his forefinger and said morosely, ''And there's something else that troubles me—this damned mess Nick Blythe's got himself embroiled in.''

Ramsey's hand jerked on his brandy glass, sending a shower of amber liquid across the table. As he mopped it up with a napkin, he said hastily, ''I fear my cousin's case is quite hopeless—the newspapers predict that if he is ever caught he will have to stand his trial for murder.''

''Pshaw,'' was the older man's disgusted reply. ''This scandal is a nine days' wonder, no more, and in time this ridiculous furor will subside. The press may have whipped the public into a lather, but who among us has not fought a duel in his time, or wanted to? It wasn't the first one and it certainly won't be the last. Everyone knows Blythe's pater was a King's man, and the Crown will never prosecute the son of one of its most prominent servants. I don't know your poor cousin very well, but for your sake—and Lady Mira's, since she will one day be related to him by marriage— I'm determined to help him. I have a deal of money, and you must have some influence—between us we should be able to reinstate him in society's good graces, before it's too late.''

''But how? No one knows where he has gone,'' Ramsey said. But his uncle hadn't heard him; a ruddy-faced gentleman had stepped forward, and the two men were already reminiscing about days long gone.

Left to his own thoughts, Ramsey stared into his glass as he considered what had happened that afternoon. He had finally screwed up his courage and called upon Georgiana, only to find that she was the merest shadow of the woman who had been his eager mistress. But even though she had seemed distant and a trifle cool, she hadn't accused him of anything. And why should she? He'd done nothing wrong. Oh, he'd tried to cloak his own sins by encouraging Sir Algernon to believe that Dominic, not he, was her ladyship's lover, but how could he have guessed that a fatal duel would be the result? Everything that happened on the following morning was shocking, regrettable, tragic, but to step forward now and confess his part would benefit no one, least of all himself.

Yet each time someone mentioned Dominic's name, Ramsey was reminded that his cousin might have to live out his life in exile. And now, just when he was beginning to think himself completely safe, his Uncle Isaac had commanded him to set everything to rights. If he succeeded, like the knights of old he would be rewarded with a fair bride and sufficient monies to reclaim his ancestral home, but no dragonslayer had ever faced a more formidable foe than his own unquiet conscience.

It might be, he thought hopefully, that by finding Dominic and helping to establish his innocence he would wipe the slate clean. But would it be possible to accomplish that without also putting his own reputation at risk? This question further depressed Ramsey's spirits, and even though he reached instinctively for the decanter, he knew that no amount of brandy could completely banish his fears of discovery and dishonour.

The following week, Ramsey visited the sale-rooms of an auction house in Tavistock Street, where a nobleman's vast library was being dispersed. He was not an avid reader, but reportedly a number of books on the turf and the chase would be offered for sale, and those he did collect in a desultory fashion. He was looking for a first edition of Beckford's *Thoughts on Hunting,* now that he could afford to indulge himself. He had already spent some of his uncle's largesse on new raiment, which had greatly improved his appearance. His hunting clothes, however well made, had never displayed his stocky, muscular figure to advantage, and it was remarkable what a clever—and expensive—tailor could achieve. On this day he sported a green swallow-tailed coat and nankeen pantaloons. He had also visited a skilled barber, who had shorn his sun-streaked brown curls and coaxed them into a flattering and fashionable crop. These changes had been wrought with an eye to pleasing that seventeen-year-old girl upon whom he had pinned his hopes, but he had not yet paid his visit to Swanborough Abbey, where, according to his uncle, she was spending the autumn. Each day he found a new excuse for putting off his intended journey to Leicestershire. During the afternoon he haunted the subscription room at Tattersall's, by night he courted the favours of a pretty opera dancer, and he spent the early hours of the morning at gaming tables of one of the many halls to be found in the neighbourhood of St. James.

Although he submitted the catalogue of books on sale to a painstaking perusal, he failed to find the one he wanted. He was on the point of leaving when the Marquis of Elston entered the sale-room, a lady in black on his arm. The couple walked past Ramsey as if they were quite oblivious to his presence, and he saw that his cousin's companion was the widowed Lady Titus. They had given him the cut indirect. Striving to maintain his composure, Ramsey was more than ever inclined to agree with his uncle that Damon was as cold-blooded as his late father, who, according to rumour, had banished his wife and only son to his country estate in order that his debauchery in town might continue unchecked. The unhappy Lovells—dubbed the Lovelesses by the London wits—had been united in death if not in life, for they met their end simultaneously, in a carriage accident.

Feigning an interest in a calf-bound book on cattle breeding, he eyed the handsome young nobleman malevolently. The marquis was drifting towards a table displaying the volumes dealing with foreign travel; Georgiana had wandered off to another part of the room. Taking advantage of her absence, Ramsey approached his relative and enquired whether he was planning a journey.

"Not any time soon," Lord Elston disclaimed in a bored voice. "But then, one never knows."

At least he had not delivered a cut direct; he was simply being his usual enigmatic self. Ramsey felt confident enough to say, "I didn't know you were so well acquainted with Lady Titus."

"My attentions are philanthropic, not amorous, dear coz. You would be surprised to know how many of her ladyship's former friends have cast her off since Sir Algernon's unfortunate demise."

Ramsey flushed, reading in this caustic remark a criticism of himself. If Georgiana had told Damon about their liaison, he would have to be very careful indeed. Thinking it best to change the subject, and quickly, he asked, "Have you seen Justin lately?"

"I regret I've not had the pleasure for several days. This week he seems to spend all his time reading briefs or following some barrister in and out of the courtrooms. But why am I telling you this, when you must surely be aware of your brother's habits?"

Ramsey, who had avoided Justin in the weeks following the party in Clifford Street, didn't care to admit that fact, certainly not to his supercilious and possibly suspicious cousin.

"By the way, Ram, I've been wondering if you've received any communication from Lord Blythe."

"I have not," Ramsey replied, more sharply than he intended.

"I daresay you are quite anxious to learn how he has fared since leaving the Metropolis."

Ramsey resented this kind of quizzing by someone so many years his junior. "I *am* concerned about Nick, and I would very much like to help him out of his present difficulties." He was pleased with this speech, and hoped his cousin would be similarly impressed.

"You astonish me," the marquis murmured, and Ramsey flinched. The deep blue eyes were hard and merciless, more so than was customary. "I did not realise that your devotion to Lord Blythe ran to such lengths. Justin, on the other hand, would give his life for the so noble Dominic. And very nearly did, a fortnight past."

"What do you mean?"

Lord Elston smiled, but not very pleasantly. "Did Justin fail to tell you of his great adventure? I never thought him a secretive fellow—unlike others I could name. Your brother acted as Blythe's second in the duel."

"You can't be serious!"

"Ask him, if you doubt my word. But you shouldn't, for I was also present."

"You?" Bemused, Ramsey shook his head. "I had no idea."

"That, dear coz, is perfectly obvious. I offered to serve as Sir Algernon's second not because I supported his accusations against my good friend Blythe, which I know to be quite false, but in order that their dispute might be kept as quiet as possible."

"But if Nick should ever stand trial, Justin might also be implicated in the case!"

"And so would I be. Though naturally I don't expect you to be much concerned with my fate," Lord Elston sighed.

But Ramsey scarcely heard him, for he was still struggling with the dread fact of his brother's involve-

ment in the duel. As his horror receded, it was
replaced by rage. He resented the fact that Dominic—
and Damon—had permitted Justin to endanger himself, and his career. But wasn't he also at fault, for
telling that damned lie about Dominic in the first
place?

"I must find my cousin," he said desperately. "Will
you help me?"

The marquis raised his malacca walking-stick and
tapped the viscount on the chest with its golden knob.
"I think, Ram, that you would do better to leave Dominic alone. Haven't you troubled him enough for one
lifetime?"

The willowy nobleman turned and walked away, and
Ramsey, thoroughly alarmed by the implication left
hanging in the air, had no opportunity to refute it.

7

THE FINE WEATHER seemed a favourable omen to Nerissa on the day Nick took her to see her new home, the farm they now invariably referred to as their Arcadia. A hired horse and gig carried them from Carlisle, whose long history of strife could be traced in the remains of her battle-scarred castle, and into the surrounding countryside. The Cumbrian mountains and moorland were no longer shrouded by the thick, low-hanging mist of the past several days, and Nerissa was charmed by the strange, stark landscape, so unlike that of her part of England. She had already learned that the north could sometimes be chilly and forbidding, and sadly damp.

During their drive on that bright morning, she was glad to see that the strain had left Nick's eyes, and his air of despondency was gone. Their alliance had effectively reduced the degree of desperation each of them had felt at various stages of their journey, he at Lutterworth and she at Leek. During their travels, he had described his ideal farm to her so many times, in such minute detail that she had easily believed it really existed, although his initial lack of success in locating it had seemed to prove otherwise. Each day he'd left their inn in Scotch Street in hopes of finding the place where they hoped to live together in peace and harmony and perfect amity, but not until yesterday had the land agent shown him Mr. Haslam's untenanted property near Wetheral, only a few miles from the city.

This hamlet, Nerissa discovered, was a cluster of houses built around a triangular common, with an ancient church set a little distance away, by the river. The main road followed the broad sweep of the Eden, and beyond the village the gig passed by the ruined gatehouse of the Benedictine priory that had once stood there. Nick reined in so she could admire the distant view of Corby Castle on the opposite bank, but she was more enthusiastic about the river itself, prompting him to say, "This affinity for water must be a legacy from your father."

"And of my mother's as well," she laughed.

"Oh? I don't think you've ever mentioned her before now."

"She died when I was but a week old," Nerissa explained, "so I know very little about her. I've always thought her name quite beautiful—Gabrielle de Tourzel. Papa met her on one of his voyages."

"Was she a Creole?"

"Goodness no," she laughed, "nothing so exotic. She came from Jersey."

"That sounds exotic to me," he said, urging the horse into a walk.

"A storm in the channel once forced my father to dock on the island, at St. Aubin harbour. During his time on shore he visited the marketplace, where he saw a beautiful red-haired girl. He was so enraptured that he followed her home and alarmed her family by requesting permission to pay his addresses. His courtship lasted as long as the storm, and by the time he sailed for Madras, they were engaged. The following year he returned to Jersey and wed her and brought her to England."

Just as her tale ended, they rounded a bend in the road that brought them to the farm. The rocky land, decorated with clumps of heather and gorse and dormant fern, was dotted with sheep and criss-crossed with drystone walls. The house of weathered stone was hardly the cottage she had envisioned, but a rambling structure at the base of a hill, dominated by a square pele tower. It lent a pleasing air of antiquity to the place and, Nick said, had been erected centuries before in defence against the Scots.

The drive was rutted from recent rains, and the stable yard, bounded by several outbuildings, was choked with mud. McNab, the wiry Scotsman who served as caretaker and farm manager, was at work laying in a supply of straw. He issued a laconic greeting and took charge of the horse and gig. Nick escorted Nerissa to the front door of the house, where they found Mrs. McNab on her knees, scrubbing the steps. More solidly built than her spouse, she possessed a sharp nose and a jutting chin, and was slightly more talkative.

"The place is a reet mess," she informed her new mistress, shaking her head. "I've sent for Sally from the village to help me put things in order, but even with two pair of hands it's a hard task."

They left her to her work, and Nick conducted Nerissa over the house himself. The rooms were irregularly sized, although the parlour was spacious enough; much of the furniture was at least two centuries old, solid and well made. Fearing that the wooden chairs with carved backs, great oaken chests, and old-fashioned settles might not be to her taste, Nick told Nerissa she had *carte blanche* to make whatever improvements seemed necessary to her. The bedchambers were more sparsely appointed, the largest with only a four-posted monstrosity hung with moth-eaten brocade.

Manfully preserving his countenance in the face of the lady's blushes, Nick commented, "A bit gloomy, don't you think? I daresay you'll prefer the tower room, which lies down the hall.''

This small, quaint chamber did indeed take Nerissa's fancy. ''But won't the servants wonder at my failure to share your quarters?'' she asked him.

''I shouldn't think so,'' he replied gravely, although his eyes were bright with amusement. ''Do you not know, Nerissa, that married persons of the Quality commonly sleep in separate bedchambers? We will be following a custom established by the highest in the land.'' Their sleeping arrangements thus established, they made their cautious way down the uneven stone steps of the spiral staircase.

A short time later, when he showed her the apple orchard behind the house, Nerissa surveyed the crop and observed, ''My first task will be to make cider—provided we can find some local lads to pick all of this ripe fruit.''

''Do you know how?'' Nick asked doubtfully as he ducked to avoid a heavily laden branch.

''I most certainly do—my Aunt Portia taught me well. I can't boast that I'm as excellent a housekeeper as she was, but I assure you I managed to keep Papa tolerably comfortable after we moved to Olney.''

He reached up to pluck an apple and took an experimental bite. Looking over at Nerissa, he smiled and said, ''So tell me, wife, what do you think of your new home?''

''I think, husband, that you have chosen well.''

''In all things,'' he murmured, his eyes on her lovely face.

But she didn't hear him; she was already composing mental lists in preparation for her assault upon the cabinetmakers, upholsterers, and china warehouses of Carlisle.

* * *

"Do you take cream in your tea, Mrs. Blythe?"

Nerissa was now so used to being addressed by the false name that her heart no longer skipped a beat every time she heard it. "No. Thank you," she answered, and stretched out her hand to receive the cup Mrs. Haslam passed to her.

She and Nick had spent the afternoon in Carlisle, and had dined at their landlord's mansion in Abbey Street. After dinner, the banker had lured Nick into his study and Nerissa, bereft of his bracing presence, had followed the lady of the house and her daughter to the drawing-room. Silently praying the gentlemen would not be long over their port, she fastened a smile upon her face and complimented Mrs. Haslam on the excellence of the tea. "Indian, is it not?" she ventured, knowing herself to be on firm ground. Her father had taught her a great deal about the commodity on which so large a part of his fortune had been founded.

"You like it?" the lady asked. "I had it from one of our local merchants." After a sip from her own cup, she leaned forward to say, "Although Maria and I are not in the habit of receiving Mr. Haslam's tenants, this time we are happy to make an exception. Maria, dear, please be so good as to shift the fire-screen for Mrs. Blythe."

Miss Maria Haslam, a tall, spare woman on the shady side of forty, obediently performed this office.

Said Mrs. Haslam, her full-moon face set in serious lines, "Truly, Mrs. Blythe, it breaks my heart to think of you stuck out on that dismal little farm. Could you not persuade your husband that a townhouse would have been more to your liking?"

"Now, Mama," Miss Haslam said warningly.

"No, Maria, I mean to speak my mind," the plump matron declared. "I know it may seem a very romantical notion, love in a cottage, and of course the poor French Queen set a fashion for that sort of thing. But the inconvenience of living at such a distance from town! You may think me a frivolous creature, Mrs. Blythe, but I would simply perish without the shops to visit and friends to call upon, to say nothing of the assemblies that are held during the Assizes!"

Her daughter gave their guest an apologetic smile, saying cheerfully, "But the farm is no more than half a dozen miles from Carlisle, Mama. You make it sound like the ends of the earth!"

"It might as well be," her parent persisted, shaking her head until her cheeks bobbled. Nerissa assured her that living in the country was no hardship. Mrs. Haslam said, "I suppose you know best," but she didn't seem convinced. "Have you had any luck hiring servants, my dear?"

"Mrs. McNab cooks for us, and Sally Willis, a girl from the village, lives in."

"Only one maid?" the older woman cried, horrified. "But I could never manage with fewer than three!" And Nerissa dared not admit that she performed a number of household tasks with her own willing and capable hands.

The conversation would have foundered at this point, had not Maria Haslam expressed her admiration of Mrs. Blythe's gown, a lovely plum-coloured silk with a lace overdress. Talk turned to the current London modes, and not long after, the gentlemen returned.

Mr. Blythe moved to his wife's side with an alacrity that caused the Haslam ladies to exchange a speaking glance. Mrs. Haslam heaved a sentimental sigh at this proof of the young husband's devotion, then said, "I hope you won't think it an impertinence, but have you and Mrs. Blythe been married long?"

Nick, standing by Nerissa's chair, placed one calming hand on her shoulder. With perfect ease—and a marvellous lack of precision—he replied, "For less than a year, ma'am."

He was conscious of a curious sense of pride when the ladies begged Nerissa to visit them often; obviously they were much taken with her. And why should they not be, he thought, for her company manners had proved to be impeccable, and no one could fault her appearance. But when, during their drive back to the farm, he tried to compliment her, he found her to be a great deal concerned with the stirrings of her conscience.

"What *fiends* we are," she said mournfully, "treating those nice people so shabbily! I think I shall never feel easy about deceiving everyone we meet."

Nick heaved a sigh that shook his large frame, and his voice was especially uneven when he said, "With all the larger sins in my dish, our pretending to be married doesn't seem to me such a terrible one." Hoping to cheer her a little, he added, "By the by, our affable landlord has swelled the ever-growing ranks of your admirers. Before we broached the first bottle of port, old Haslam said heartily, if rather inelegantly, that I was a lucky young dog. And naturally I agreed with him."

This comment failed to win him the smile he had counted on. His occasional gallantries inevitably fell flat—as puzzling as it was disappointing. And their initial foray into local society had left her so dispirited that he knew it was not an auspicious moment to begin the seduction that was increasingly on his mind.

He owed her his life, he was fully conscious of it, but shorn as he was of title and estate, he had very little to offer by way of recompense. At least, he reflected, he could provide her with the security of a permanent home, and with that in mind he had mentioned to Mr. Haslam that he was interested in purchasing the freehold of Arcadia Farm. The canny old banker, knowing the amount his tenant, also his client, kept on deposit, had named a figure so large that Nick declined to meet it. But at least the bargaining had begun, and soon he must write Cat Durham and recover the money he had left with her.

When they arrived home, Nick bid Nerissa his usual polite, impersonal good-night in the upstairs hall, and they entered their respective apartments.

Nerissa had made her tower room a cosy place, but it was drafty nonetheless, and she quickly changed into her nightshift and dressing gown, a handsome, gaudy garment of blue silk with bamboo leaves picked out in gold thread. She sat down to brush and braid her hair, and as she dropped the combs and pins into her lap she wished, not for the first time, that she had been blessed with her friend Laura's smooth, blonde tresses. Unbound, her heavy chestnut mane turned her into that wild gypsy girl her father had so often called her.

She had not troubled to lock her door, for Nick had never sought entry to her room, so when she heard a soft knock, she experienced a frisson of panic. After a moment of indecision, she tied the corded sash more tightly about her waist and called, "Come in." To her own ears the invitation sounded tentative at best.

He was still fully dressed, she was relieved to see, and his purpose in coming was to bring her a book she had purchased that afternoon in Carlisle. "McNab found this in the gig," he said, placing it on a table.

This reminded her of something she had forgotten to tell him earlier. "There is a registry office next to the bookseller's," she said, "and persons seeking employment sometimes gather at the area railing and accost the passers-by. Today I was approached by a young man—a boy, really, for he can't be more than seventeen. He had the reddest hair I've ever seen, and wanted to know if I required a footman. It was all I could do to keep from laughing, for he was so young, and *so* shabby, but I told him there might be work for him here.''

"If you are bent on hiring on a manservant, you would do better to hire a trained one than some stray cub," Nick said.

"I don't like footmen, they don't seem human to me. Besides, any decent one would hold up his nose at our menage." She picked up her brush and plied it with such vigour that her hair crackled. "This Alec Hewes had an honest face, and he's country bred. He might be useful for odd jobs like carpentry or looking after the cows. And I expect Mrs. McNab would like having someone to order about besides Sally—she has such an autocratic disposition."

Nick, who had been wandering about the room, paused to pick up her silver hand-mirror from the dressing table. Running his forefinger over the initials engraved upon its back, he asked her what the R signified.

"Rosalind. Nerissa Rosalind."

"The captain must have been exceedingly fond of the Bard."

"It happens that he was, but he was obliged to name me for one of Shakespeare's ladies—it's a tradition in his family," Nerissa told him. "His sister was Portia and his mother was Beatrice, and his aunts were Viola and Ophelia—oh, it goes back for generations. I have always been thankful for the names I was given. I might easily have been called something quite horrid, like Hippolyta or Calpurnia."

"Or Goneril." He looked over at her, frowning slightly. "I believe there is a noble family that follows the same custom."

Nerissa, knowing all too well which noble family he meant, suddenly averted her eyes. "How very interesting, to be sure."

Should she reveal her connection to the Duke of Solway? She considered this, but in the end rejected the notion. She and Nick had met as equals, and she preferred that they continue as such. To tell him that she was related to the Marchant clan—and was an heiress besides—would serve no good purpose, and it might conceivably damage their easy relationship. At present her aristocratic kinsman played no part in her life, and her inheritance was held in trust until her marriage, or her twenty-fifth birthday, a full eighteen months away. Being quite unaffected by both circumstances, she could see no reason why she should admit to either.

Nick broke the quiet by saying, "I must cull *The Merchant of Venice* for suitable quotations to address to you. Did you remember to purchase a set of Shakespeare at the bookseller's?"

"Among other things," she replied in a voice of doom. "I'm afraid I've run up quite a bill in the name of Mrs. Nicholas Blythe of Arcadia Farm, Wetheral. Who doesn't even exist."

"No, she certainly does not," he agreed. "My parents, less literary minded than yours, christened me Dominic."

Her hairbrush paused in midstroke, and she eyed him accusingly. "You might have told me!"

"I'm sorry, I forgot you didn't know. You needn't call me Dominic if you don't like it," he said, amused by her fierce expression.

"It isn't the *name* I dislike, but the not knowing." She began to plait her hair, biting her lower lip in concentration, and forgot her momentary annoyance.

Nick watched this operation in silence, and when it was over he said teasingly, "I never guessed that the night transformed you into a mandarin, pigtail and all."

Without looking up at him she said, "My robe belonged to a mandarin—or so Papa always said. I was never entirely sure he was telling the truth."

"It is vastly becoming, wherever it came from."

When he was gone, Nerissa considered this new habit of making such personal remarks. At times he seemed to be pursuing something more than a platonic friendship, although he had yet to say or do anything that could be construed as an advance. He would, of that she was certain. But she was experienced in fending off amorous gentlemen, she thought with some pride, and was both fully prepared and perfectly able to do so.

"Unseemly, I call it," Mrs. McNab grumbled as she surveyed the wreck of her kitchen, littered with pots and pans and utensils. "Why should decent, godly folk want to build bonfires, I'd like to know?"

Sally Willis, a pretty country girl with dusky curls and pink cheeks, paused on her way to the scullery to say shyly, "Alec said it's to fright the witches." She brushed back a lock of dark hair, her hand white with flour.

Nerissa laughed, but she hastened to correct this false impression. "He was thinking of All Hallow's Eve. Tonight, we'll be honouring—or rather, *dis*honouring—Guy Fawkes, the Catholic gentleman who conspired with others of his religion to blow up Parliament." She opened the door of the bread oven to remove the first of two apple pies, using a dishcloth to protect her hands from the hot plate.

"And for that we must go to all this trouble and encourage the farm folk to roister all the night?" Mrs. McNab fumed. She cast a darkling glance at the kitchenmaid and said bitterly, "And Sally forgetting to dust the downstairs rooms because she spent all morning sewing a big dolly and stuffing it with straw! Heathenish doings, mistress, and I like it not!"

"Part of the fun is burning Guy in effigy," Nerissa explained. As she reached for the second pie, her cloth slipped, and when her palm touched the edge of the tin, she jerked it back with a cry of pain.

"Now you've gone and burned yourself over this foolishness," the Scotswoman said, aggrieved. "Sit you down, mistress, I've a certain remedy. Sally, lass, fetch me the alum powder and some water—be quick, now!"

She mixed a paste which she applied to Nerissa's wound. "You needn't bind it," she said gruffly, "and the pain will go off soon, or my name's not Martha McNab. Rest ye easy, there's nothing more needs doing that Sally and I can't manage between us."

Nerissa reminded Sally to fetch two bottles of claret from the cellar and gather together the spices Nick required for the punch he insisted upon making, before hurrying to her room to dress for the simple country fête, her first in her new home. Not knowing which of her gowns was Nick's favourite, she put on her grey silk, and in honour of the occasion unearthed a pair of kid dancing slippers and bound her hair with cherry ribbons.

At dusk the company began to straggle in, and a handsome feast was laid out upon the dining-room table. After everyone was wonderfully stuffed with mutton, parsnips, baked custards, and pie—all washed down with liberal doses of ale—Nick announced it was time to repair to the top of the hill.

Alec Hewes had built a bonfire of such startling proportions that upon seeing it, Nerissa observed that it would likely take all night to burn away. "I shouldn't be surprised," Nick replied with a laugh, before going to take the torch from the young man. He kindled the vast pile of wood, and as soon as the fire was well established, the cloth and straw figure of Sally's making was strung to a long pole and held over the leaping flames. The children watched, open mouthed, as the effigy was consumed, but seeing that their elders laughed and clapped, they followed suit.

As the children capered about, chasing each other and shouting gleefully, Nerissa thought of Samuel, and a seemingly distant time when her days had been filled with the sweet sounds of lullaby and baby's cry.

When the party returned to the house, Alec Hewes said to her, " 'Tis a treat the wee bairns won't soon forget, mistress.''

''They wouldn't have had it if you hadn't built such a grand bonfire,'' she replied. The grass on the steep hillside was already coated with frost; it crackled beneath the soles of her slippers, and although she made her way cautiously, she very nearly lost her footing. The young man reached out to take her arm, preventing a fall, and when she turned her head to thank him she was startled by his besotted expression. He mumbled something unintelligible and suddenly bolted, half running and half stumbling down the hill. At that moment Nick stepped out of the shadows, and she greeted him thankfully and a trifle desperately.

''Another admirer, Nerissa?'' In the wavering torchlight she could not read his face, but she guessed it was disapproving. ''Come along,'' she heard him say, ''you should not be standing out in the cold.''

Their company reassembled in the parlour, which Nerissa had rendered more comfortable by removing the straight-backed settle and wooden stools and replacing them with a cosy sofa and several wing chairs. The men shoved these against the wall to make room for dancing and rolled up the fine Turkey carpet that was her pride and joy. When Mr. McNab took up his instrument, everyone cried out for the master and mistress to begin the dancing. Nerissa let Nick lead her onto the floor before it occurred to her that he had never partnered her before, which might well be obvious to the onlookers.

"As we are unacquainted with the northern reels," he said, "perhaps we had best let the locals show us the way. Alec, Sally," he called over his shoulder, "Mrs. Blythe and I cannot manage this business without you."

The little maidservant blushed rosily and Alec swallowed, his Adam's apple rising and falling. But the younger couple heeded their employer's command, and to the accompaniment of the pipes they executed a simple step. Nerissa linked hands with Nick and they joined in, tentatively at first, laughing at their mistakes, but with every measure they grew more confident. The warm glow of the candles and the firelight softened the harsh planes of his face, easing the lines of tension about his eyes and mouth, and Nerissa forgot that he and she were no more married than Alec and Sally. He swung her around with dizzying speed, and she let out a most undignified shriek. And when the reel ended, she collapsed against his broad chest, breathless from exertion.

"You dance very well, wife," he whispered, before releasing her.

At his invitation, the others joined in the dancing. He busied himself with concocting the punch, while Nerissa sat down at the hearthside with the young people to roast chestnuts. More food was served—and more drink—and the party did not break up until midnight, by which time the children were half asleep and their fathers none so steady on their feet. When everyone had gone, Nerissa dismissed Sally to her garret room and sent a yawning Alec to his bed above the stables, which he shared with the brown-and-white rat terrier which kept the place free of vermin. Then she repaired to the silent kitchen to tidy up. She had just locked the meat safe when Nick entered the room, a pewter tankard in hand.

"Best have a care," she warned him, "else your

head will pay the price tomorrow." She reached out to take the vessel from him and her long sleeve fell back, exposing the red mark on her hand.

"What've you done to yourself?"

"It's a trifling burn—Mrs. McNab rubbed some salve on it, and it doesn't even hurt now."

He shook his head at her. "What a one you are for getting into trouble."

Something in his comment seemed to her to go beyond her injury and she blurted, "I wasn't flirting with Alec tonight."

"I never suggested that you had been."

"But you must have been thinking it," she said unhappily.

"Oh, no," he replied, his eyes dark with some emotion she could not quite define, "I've been too busy thinking how very much I would like for you to flirt with *me.*" He placed his hands on either side of her face and drew it towards him. His mouth, she discovered, tasted of oranges and spices and wine, and his kiss was more intoxicating than the punch he had imbibed so freely. Gradually, without her being aware of it, her fingers uncurled from the handle of the tankard, until it slipped free and fell to the floor with a loud clatter.

For several seconds they stared at one another with a new awareness, and the only sound in the room was the faint hiss of the banked fire.

Nick stared down at his hands, lost in the thickness of her hair; the dark tendrils curled around his fingers as if to bind him to her. He said ruefully, "I've never done this in a kitchen before."

"Done what?" she asked witlessly.

"Seduced a lady. For that, you know," he said in his foggy voice, "is exactly what I am doing." He took a deep breath, then quoted softly. " 'The first interrogatory that my Nerissa shall be sworn on is, whether till the next night she had rather stay, or go to bed now, being two hours to day.' "

"You are drunk," she sighed.

"Not at all, or I'd never have managed a speech like that one. I've been waiting for just the right moment to use it, but to speak more plainly, will you lie with me tonight, sweet Nerissa?"

She took a backward step. "I'm not your wife." But how lovely if she could be, for then there would be no shame in his invitation. "It isn't part of the arrangement," she reminded him.

"True," he agreed, "but I hoped you might be interested in renegotiating the terms. If not, then I must be patient a little while longer."

When he turned to go she realised, belatedly, that he had received the impression that someday she would be willing. She wanted to call out to him that she would never, ever change her mind, but the words stuck in her throat and remained unspoken.

It was a good thing, Nerissa told herself as she scrambled into her clothes one cold morning, that she did not mind keeping early hours. At Arcadia, she generally left her bed at the rise of the sun, and returned to it only an hour or two after supper. She was occupied every minute of the day, but as she often told Nick when he took her to task for working so hard, she simply didn't have enough time to feel tired.

After all of these days and weeks living with Nick Blythe, she knew virtually nothing of his history, or what family he had left behind. Although they slept beneath the same roof and ate at the same board like any married couple, they were wholly independent of one another. She kept busy within the house; he accompanied Mr. McNab on his daily rounds. They shared a life, but nothing of themselves. It was as if they were both waiting for some outside force to tear down the barrier they had erected, by tacit consent, on the night of the bonfire, when she had stepped out of his arms.

She put on a practical kerseymere gown and coiled her hair at the nape of her neck, all the while comparing the still mysterious Dominic to her worthy, respectable Andrew, and concluded that she much preferred being a pretend Mrs. Blythe to a lawful Mrs. Hudgins. Her existence had never been sufficiently ordered by the rules of society, by considerations of convention and propriety, for her to miss them now. The safe path had never held any charms for her. If it had, she would not be living in an isolated Cumbrian farmhouse with a man she had known slightly less than a month.

When she hurried down the spiral staircase, ready to begin the tasks of the day, she found Nick standing in the hallway. "Good morning, Mrs. Blythe," he said, his eyes dancing as they always did when he called her by that name. "I didn't expect to see you abroad so early."

"There's cider to be made, and I wouldn't want to miss the fun," she said, so much like an eager child for a promised treat that he laughed. "Will you be away all day?"

"Only for the morning—there's a prize bull on show at Warwick village, and McNab wants to look him over. Why don't you pack up some bread and cheese for a picnic—we can walk over to the caves when I return. At this season, we can't expect too many more fine days." And with a wave, he was off.

Nerissa spent her morning in the cellar, supervising Alec's labours with the ancient apple press. The young man's violent infatuation showed no signs of abating; she suspected his feelings alarmed him far more than they did her. Trusting to time to effect a cure, she was careful to treat him with a combination of kindness and disinterest.

At noon an excited Sally called her upstairs to receive a visitor.

"Pray forgive my intrusion, Mrs. Blythe," Miss Maria Haslam said when Nerissa entered the parlour.

"It is a welcome one," Nerissa said cordially. "Mrs. McNab has put the kettle on, and we shall have tea and cake directly. Today we have begun making the cider, and I fear the place is much disordered as a result."

"I quite understand. Is Mr. Blythe at home today? I think he will be particularly interested to hear what I have come to tell you, for I know how closely gentlemen follow the progress of the war."

"He and Mr. McNab have gone to Warwick to inspect a bull. Do you have news—have our armies lost a battle?"

"I cannot say, but the Navy has lately won an engagement against the French fleet, off Cape Trafalgar." The spinster's voice sank when she said, "Yet this longed-for victory came at a terrible cost. My dear, our gallant Lord Nelson was killed!"

Nerissa felt as though she'd just been told of the death of someone she had known well, and even loved.

"It happened a fortnight ago—I should have brought you Papa's paper, which told the number of ships involved and explained the particulars of the engagement, but in my haste to leave the house I left it behind."

It was just as well, Nerissa thought; a newspaper never had any good effect upon Nick's spirits. "I will tell Mr. Blythe when he returns from Warwick," she said. "You were very kind to remember us, Miss Haslam."

The other lady's dark eyes were lit with their characteristic twinkle when she said, "Oh, I often think of you, Mrs. Blythe. And, I might add, with considerable envy. You live here in this grand ruin, which I confess I have always adored, and you are exceedingly fortunate in your choice of a husband. I can't think when my father has taken such a fancy to anyone as he did to Mr. Blythe.''

This speech gratified Nerissa, but it embarrassed her, too. Fortunately she was saved the trouble of a reply by Sally, who carried in the tray. As the two ladies nibbled seed-cake and drank their tea, the conversation become more general and less personal. Nerissa's guest requested a tour of the house, and expressed her admiration of the kitchen and the still-room.

Before climbing into her carriage, Miss Haslam said warmly, ''I do hope you will visit us in Abbey Street very soon, Mrs. Blythe. Not only am I eager to repay your hospitality—I should very much like for us to be friends.''

But Nerissa knew the risk of developing a close relationship with any stranger, even one as well meaning as Maria Haslam; familiarity might breed carelessness. The lie she was forced to live had closed her off from all others save her fellow conspirator, and she could never let down her guard, not in front of her servants and certainly not with the daughter of their landlord. She accepted the hand the other lady held out to her but did not commit herself to anything, saying only, ''You are very kind.'' And she made a silent vow to stay away from Carlisle.

Later that day, when she and Nick set out on their excursion, she told him what little she knew of the naval battle, but he had already heard the news. ''They were talking of nothing else at Warwick,'' he told her. ''The whole nation is mourning the hero.''

''And well they should,'' she sighed, pulling her wool shawl closer about her shoulders. ''Poor Lady

Hamilton, I wonder what will be her fate now she has lost her Lord Nelson? People speak ill of her, but I think she is very much to be pitied now.''

Their exploration of St. Constantine's Cells, as the locals called the three caves cut into the sandstone bank of the Eden, was brief. Although they found that it was possible to stand and move about each of the manmade chambers, the dark and the cold were unpleasant. ''I should have brought a lantern,'' said Nick when they emerged.

He spread a horse blanket in a pool of sunshine on the ridge overlooking the river, and Nerissa looked up from unwrapping their meal to enquire, ''Why were the caves built?''

''No one seems to know who was originally responsible,'' he replied, ''but I believe they were sometimes used to conceal the priory's plate and money whenever the Scots raiders came calling.''

After breaking a piece of bread from the loaf she passed it to him. ''This is such a quiet part of the world that it's hard to conceive of so much pillaging and plundering going on here. Those must have been exciting times,'' she said wistfully.

''I wonder how excited you'd have been if Bonaparte had successfully invaded our shores last year?''

She laughed and acknowledged, ''Not very—I was as terrified as everyone else. I suppose the distance of time makes the past infinitely more romantic than the present.'' When he handed her the jug in exchange for the loaf, she held it up to her lips and drank. The ale was bitter, but pleasantly so, and it brought back happy memories. ''When we first moved to the country, Papa and I used to play at being gypsies, and often ate our dinner on the ground. We would walk by the river and talk for hours and hours, till the sun went down. My aunt spent the latter part of her life teaching me to be a lady, but he managed to undo all her hard work in a very short time!'' She looked out at the river, its rippling waters gilded by the Midas touch of the sun. ''I still cannot accustom myself to his being gone.''

''I know something of what you must feel,'' Nick told her, ''for I lost my own father last year.'' When she looked over at him in surprise, he said, ''Nerissa, you must learn to look to the future, not the past, if you hope to be happy. I offer myself as your tutor—and let this be your first lesson.'' He took her chin in his hand and gave her a swift, hard kiss on the mouth. He would have ended with that, but gazing into her eyes, so deeply blue that he fancied himself drowning in them, he felt the stirring of desire. ''You smell of apples,'' he murmured, before kissing her again. And when she turned her face away, he said, his voice thick with passion, ''Do not deny me—this is what you were made for, you know.''

Taking her by the shoulders, he pressed her gently down to the ground, and began to peel back her shawl before drawing her back into his embrace. But when he felt the wetness of her cheek and tasted the salt of her tears, he could not go on. Looking down at her, he realised that this was no token show of reluctance. He had known her in many moods, but never before had he seen such despair in her face. ''I'm sorry,'' he said quietly. ''I didn't mean to frighten you.''

Nerissa drew several laboured breaths. ''It isn't your fault,'' she panted. ''I knew, the day I accepted your offer of protection, that this was inevitable. I'm not afraid of you, Nick, and in truth I like you very well, but—''

''But you prefer to be admired from a distance,'' he finished for her.

He rolled over onto his back and stared up at the blue dome of the sky. She was so temptingly made, with her provocative face and generous form, but she was still not ready to accept him as a lover. For the first time he began to wonder whether she would ever be able to do so. This partnership of theirs seemed to be so seriously flawed that it might never flourish in the way he had originally hoped. He wasn't even sure how he could continue living with a woman who was so eminently desirable and at the same time so devilishly elusive.

He supposed he would have to resign himself to her stubborn determination to withhold the secrets of her body, but he could not permit her to close her mind against him. Her quietude was thoughtful rather than sulky, but he was troubled by it nonetheless and for the rest of the afternoon he exerted himself to put her to ease again.

That night after dinner they retired to the cosy parlour, according to their habit. When Nick went to the secretaire to begin his long-overdue letter to Cat Durham, Nerissa curled up on the settee and hid her face between the marbled covers of a book. Nick recognised it as one of a set of four she had bought for herself in Carlisle, a collection of the writings of Mary Wollstonecraft, and he could appreciate why she might find solace in it. Like Nerissa, the authoress had been characterised by independence and intelligence, and she had flouted convention by living with a gentleman who was not her husband. And, he thought as he trimmed his quill, Mary had also borne a child out of wedlock.

When he heard her get up, he looked around to ask, "Going upstairs so soon?"

"It is well past my usual time, as you would know if you'd looked at the clock lately." Her eyes followed him anxiously when he vacated his chair and came towards her.

"Do not worry, I am not going to do anything improper, I promise." She permitted him to kiss her cheek, and just to make her blush, he said, "You *still* smell of apples."

And then, hoping he had proved that he was a man of his word, he went back to the desk to finish his letter.

8

ONE AFTERNOON NERISSA devoted her full attention to refurbishing Nick's chamber, for ever since coming to Arcadia he had complained that the dust-heavy brocade curtains gave him sneezing fits in the night. As she vigourously pulled the rings from the old ones, she reflected that if there had been any danger of his interrupting her work, she would have postponed it indefinitely, for there was no telling what he might do if he chanced upon her in such proximity to his bed.

Before hanging the blue damask curtains she and Sally Willis had sewn, she polished the intricately carved bedposts. When she set her cloth impregnated with beeswax on a walnut chest of drawers, she noted that it cried out for similar treatment. First she had to remove a collection of Nick's personal belongings—an empty tobacco pouch, scraps of paper, a silver button which she recognised as belonging to his dress coat, and a letter. Setting these aside, she rubbed the wood until it threatened to blind her with its shine, then she replaced each item where she had found it. The letter, a single sheet, was not folded, and she could see that the writing was neat and regular—very feminine, in fact—and it bore a St. Albans postmark.

Curious to know the identity of his correspondent, she hunted for the signature. The closing words of the final paragraph leapt up at her: ''Your past kindnesses to me have been so much greater than I deserve, and there is nothing you cannot ask. Be easy, you shall have your thousand pounds as soon as I can contrive to get them to you, and more if you need it. I trust and pray you are well, and that no great hardship prompted the request of your funds, which I am happy to restore to you. I remain, as ever, your devoted Cat.''

Nerissa couldn't bring herself to read anymore; she dared not, knowing it was wrong. It was bad enough to know that in St. Albans there lived a woman named Cat who had control of Nick's money. Was she a relation, some sister or a cousin to whom he had applied for assistance? Try though she might—try though she did—she could not shove aside her fear that the relationship was other than a familial one. Perhaps this Cat was a sweetheart or a mistress he had left behind. And then it came to her with heart-stopping clarity, and the letter fell from her fingers, fluttering to the floor.

Dominic Blythe was a married man.

Her fledgling hope that he might someday make her his wife curled up and died, and in that moment she also discovered, to her shame, that she had fallen so deeply and desperately in love with him that the simple, dreadful truth of his marriage could not alter her feelings. To him she had only been a prospective mistress, and she could never expect to be anything more. Casting her mind back to that night in Leek, when he had asked her to come north with him, she recalled his frankness about his inability to offer matrimony. She might have asked him why, but instead she had acted with her usual impulsiveness, flinging herself headlong down the road to ruin.

She hurried from his room, stepping blindly past the pile of discarded brocade curtains, and made her way to her own chamber. When she had wrapped herself in a warm, protective cloak, she left the house steathily, without alerting any of the servants, and walked towards the river. To get there she had to cut across a meadow where sheep grazed; the animals darted nervously out of her way. The day had been particularly fine, but now the sun had begun its westerly descent, leaving behind long streaks of pink and orange on the pale azure palette overhead. Nerissa trudged on, heedless alike of the brambles that caught at her skirts and the wind which swept along the fells and across the moors.

Of all the many trials she had undergone in the months since her father's death, this was surely the worst. She longed for a broad masculine shoulder to rest her head upon, but Nick's was denied her. She needed someone to talk to, but she had no other friend. And however much she might love him, she could not continue living with him—nor could she bring herself to admit that she had seen his wife's letter. She would encourage him to believe that she was weary of the deception, and so bored by their restricted life that she had made up her mind to go to London after all.

The advance of dusk was swift and merciless, and in minutes the world changed from brilliant gold to dismal grey. Nerissa drew her cloak more tightly about her and sat down upon a rock at the edge of the water.

Mary Wollstonecraft had been correct when she wrote that nothing destroyed peace of mind more than platonic attachments. Nerissa was now convinced of her favourite author's assertion that such relationships often ended in sorrow; having succumbed to that "dangerous tenderness" Mary had alluded to, she could no longer be satisfied by mere friendship with Nick Blythe. Her traitorous heart had not remained disengaged, and on the day of their picnic at the caves her treacherous passions had been stirred. His skilled and seductive assault upon her person had been nothing like Andrew's tentative demonstrations of affection, and it had answered many questions about who she was and what she wanted in a lover. For a brief, lovely moment she had given in to that wild, wanton creature dwelling inside her, whose existence she had never intended to reveal to any man, least of all to Nick. When tempted, her salvation had not been her conscience but that stronger fear of becoming what the people of Olney had called her.

In time, she might have given herself to him, in the expectation that she would one day be his bride. He was a man of honour, and she believed he would have wed her had there been no impediment to a legal union. She felt she was more truly his wife than the woman who had expressed her devotion so sweetly yet hadn't had the decency to accompany him into exile. The real Mrs. Blythe was safe in St. Albans, with plenty of money at her disposal, and whatever she might be suffering, it was Nick who had paid the higher price—banishment, no less.

The discovery that night had fallen heavily around her startled Nerissa out of her abstraction, and when she walked slowly homeward, the path before her was barely visible and the noises of the countryside seemed louder because of the darkness. A sheep's cough made her jump, and there was an ominous rustling in the reeds along the river. But it was only the brown-and-white terrier which seldom strayed very far from Alec's side, and Nerissa, glancing over her shoulder, saw the young man following behind and paused to let him catch up. "Shouldn't you have been home a long time ago?" she asked. "I hope Mrs. McNab saved you some supper."

"She gave me leave to go 'cross the river," he assured her. "The ferry was delayed, or I would not be so late in coming home from the castle. I heard they may be hiring on a new groom, and went to enquire." The youth whistled to the dog; it scurried up the bank.

"Mr. Blythe would be very sorry to lose you," Nerissa said kindly as Alec fell into step beside her.

He ducked his head self-consciously, avoiding her eye. "The master has been good to me, but I've been thinking it might be best to find me a new place."

She hadn't believed she could feel any worse, but knowing that his guilt over his attachment to her compelled him to leave Nick's employ depressed her spirits even further. "Oh, Alec," she said, and the words came out as a mournful sigh.

"Mistress?"

"Don't—don't make up your mind too hastily." She couldn't tell him she was leaving; he would hear about it soon enough. But now there was yet another reason not to delay her departure from Arcadia Farm.

Mrs. McNab gave Nick the news of Nerissa's disappearance when he returned from his day in town. His mood was not the best, for none of his business there had been successful. The chaise he had ordered from the Carlisle carriage-maker was not yet ready, and he had failed to find a suitable pair of horses at an auction. His landlord still demanded a purchase price that he knew to be far in excess of what the farm was worth. Now Nerissa had gone missing—it only needed that, he thought morosely as he stood at the parlour window, watching and waiting and worrying. His vigil ended when two figures approached the house, with a small dog tagging at their heels.

"Where the devil have you been?" he growled at Nerissa when she stepped into the room. No sooner had he spoken the rough question than he wished he could call it back, because it sent the colour flying from her cheeks. Her pallor made her eyes seem even more blue, and the black mole stood out starkly against her white skin.

"I—I went for a walk by the river," she faltered.

"I never meant to be so late returning." She went to kneel before the fire, and after a moment looked up and asked him to close the door. "There is something I must say to you, in private."

When he had complied with her request, he sat down in his favourite chair, saying lightly, "I hope you aren't about to tell me that you're planning to run off with the stableboy."

She closed her eyes, her expression one of anguish, then opened them again. Staring at the dancing flames, she said quietly, "No, not that. But I *am* going away. I simply cannot go on living here, pretending to be what I am not. Once I thought I could, but I was mistaken."

Nick abruptly abandoned his chair. "Nerissa, I would never harm you, surely you know that. Are you so afraid of me?"

"More afraid of myself, I think. But we are neither of us saints."

"That we are not," he agreed, holding her so close that he could feel her breasts rise and fall against his chest as she laboured for breath. "Don't go," he whispered.

"It's no good," she said, although she made no attempt to break away. "You won't change my mind with a few kisses and a caress or two. Remember, before we ever began this charade, you said I would be free to end my part in it at any time."

But he didn't want to be held to some rash promise he'd made so many weeks ago, before he had grown to depend upon her—to love her. For a long time now he had desired her, but it was possible to want a woman without really knowing her. It was the knowing that made all the difference.

When she stepped out of his embrace, she continued, "I have a cousin in London, the Duke of Solway.

He is a good-hearted man, so perhaps he will not judge me too harshly when I throw myself upon his mercy.''

"The Duke of Solway,'' he repeated. "How can you possibly be related—I thought your father was a sea captain?''

The corners of her mouth lifted in a smile. "Even a sea captain can come from a ducal house. My grandmother was Lady Beatrice Marchant, for all she married a plain Mr. Newby. Papa was first cousin to the present duke, and the two were excellent friends as well.'' Nerissa wandered over to the window to draw the curtains, and when she was done she faced Nick again and said, "You mustn't think I am intimate with the Marchants, for nothing could be less true. They go in for hunting and balls and other pursuits for which my father had no time or interest, but sometimes he took me with him to Haberdine Castle in Northamptonshire. The duchess was so toplofty she scared me half to death, and Gervase and Edgar and Ophelia and Imogen were always racing about on their ponies. They deemed me very poor company, and I think in their eyes I was a little tainted by my father's trade. But Cousin William—the duke—was always very kind to me, and I hope he will be again.''

If Nick had doubted her, which he didn't, the way she rattled off these names and titles would have convinced him of her claim. Her very name, taken from Shakespeare, was proof of her tie to the Marchants. Nevertheless, it was disconcerting to discover that this daughter of an obscure merchant seaman was related to one of the noblest families in the realm. "Why didn't you tell me before now?'' he asked her.

"I didn't want you to misunderstand, to think me something I am not. I've never moved in the same exalted sphere as my cousins do, nor will I do so in future.'' Moving towards the door, she said, "I mean to leave for Haberdine in a few days. I'll have to think

up some plausible excuse to explain my sudden departure . . . a sick relative or something." She prevented
further discussion by saying hurriedly, "Pray excuse
me, but I am tired from my walk. Mrs. McNab has
made some soup—could you tell Sally that I'd like
some brought up to me in a bit?"

Privacy Dominic would grant her, but never her
freedom, he told himself as the door closed behind
her. The prospect of living at Arcadia without her, of
doing anything at all without her, was insupportable.
He had lost too much already—his title, his friends,
his property—and he would not lose her too. For none
of those things he had formerly valued so highly had
any worth at all when set against the lady he was determined to keep by his side.

Nerissa, kneeling on the damp stone floor of the
cellar, placed her ear to the wooden cider cask and
listened carefully. When she heard the faint hiss from
within she looked over at Sally, standing on the top
step. "Yes," she said, "fermentation has begun. Tell
Alec it's time for him to rack the juice off into another
cask, and remind him that when he pours, he must be
very careful not to disturb the dregs."

The maidservant vanished, and Nerissa climbed to
her feet, wiping her hands on a skirt that was already
soiled from her labours in the dairy and the poultry-
yard and the kitchen. Keeping busy was the best way
to keep her sorrows at bay, so she had thrown herself
into the role of housewife with even greater fervour
than she had done formerly. Two days had passed since
she had told Nick of her plans, and only two more
remained before she would leave this house forever.
Picking up her taper, she lit her way up the steps, and
mentally ticked the task she had just performed off her
list of things to do. Time to move on to the next one:
the household mending.

She was startled when, upon emerging from the dark depths of the cellar, she came face to face with Nick. He had left for Carlisle immediately after breakfast, and usually he did not return until late. He was, she noted, dressed in his newest and best clothes, a dark coat and oyster-coloured breeches. "I'm taking you on an outing," he announced. "Run upstairs and comb those cobwebs out of your hair, and put on a fresh gown. A blue one, I think, to match your eyes. Hurry now, we haven't got all day!"

"Oh, very well," she said, poised between frustration and curiosity. "Are we going to visit Hadrian's Wall?" She had expressed this desire more than a week ago, but he had apparently forgotten it.

"Ask me no questions, I'll tell you no lies."

Her blue gown was sadly wrinkled, so she put on a white one instead, fulfilling the spirit of Nick's request by covering it with her blue pelisse. When she went back downstairs, she found him in the hall. As he held the front door open for her, he nodded approvingly and murmured, "White—now why didn't *I* think of that?"

She had assumed that they would take the gig, but there was a neat chaise and a pair of horses waiting at the door, along with a postboy in drab livery. "Did you hire it in Carlisle?" she asked.

"Only the horses," he answered, handing her into the vehicle, which smelled of leather. "I've purchased the chaise."

"Oh, Nick, such extravagance will ruin you!" It was really none of her business, so she said nothing more, but as the carriage lurched forward, it occurred to her that the money must have come from his wife.

They followed the road to Carlisle, proving wrong her guess about Hadrian's Wall, and beyond the city they passed a flat, barren stretch of land where the only dwellings were rudely built of sod and wattle.

"Where *are* we going?" she asked, and when he refused to enlighten her she heaved an exasperated sigh and turned her head towards the window to gaze at the golden sands and grey water.

"That is Solway Firth," Nick said. "From which your kinsman takes his title?"

"No, it came from the Border town of Solway Moss. There was a battle, in the sixteenth century, I think, and the Marchant of the day distinguished himself in the fighting and was ennobled as a result. Papa used to tell me the story when I was a child." She wondered if her ancestor had been as struck by the bleakness of the flat marshland as she was.

"We are very nearly in Scotland, and the next town on this road is Gretna Green. That being the case, perhaps you might like to take part in the most popular local custom?" When she turned an astonished face upon him, Nick smiled and said, "I'm asking you if you will marry me, and I do hope you'll agree, or else I've abducted you to no purpose."

As the import of this speech became clear to her, Nerissa went rigid with shock. What he suggested was an abomination—how could he be so callously cruel, so utterly shameless? "You must be mad!" she gasped.

"I've never been more serious in my life."

Hot fury mobilised her and she drew back her arm to strike him, a futile attempt, for he caught her hand just before it connected with his cheek. "Let me go, damn you!" she cried. "Do you expect me to say I am *honoured* by your proposal? What you suggest is hateful, disgusting! It would be bigamy!" She tried to pull free of him, but his grip on her tightened.

"You are *married?* For God's sake, answer me, Nerissa!"

Cowed by the dangerous glitter in his eyes, she shook her head. "Not I—you."

During her disjointed explanation about finding the letter, Nick's face gradually regained its colour, and the wild light died out of his eyes. "You didn't read very much of it, did you?" he said when she fell silent. "Because if you had, you'd know that Cat is *not* my wife."

If he lied, he was a master of the art, because his words rang with sincerity. Nerissa eyed him uncertainly. "Who is she, then?"

"For most of the years I've known her, she was my father's mistress. But she has also been my friend. After the duel I stayed the night at her house in St. Albans and entrusted some of my funds to her keeping. Our correspondence has been financial, not amorous." He smiled over at Nerissa as he said warmly, "My dear, I am so much a bachelor that I have never even come close to offering marriage to any lady. Until today."

"Yet not so long ago you said you could never marry me," she reminded him.

"You are wondering why I've changed my mind?" he asked, leaning close to her. "I think you'll agree that this is reason enough."

While he kissed her, she could not think, and when he stopped, his husky words rendered all thought unnecessary.

"Nerissa, why should we continue to live a lie when a simple exchange of words can make us honest? In your heart you must know this is right—and I have decided it is time." As the chaise jolted across a bridge, its pace slowed, and Nick said, "The fame of this place is such that the postboy will think nothing of our stopping here—fully half of Gretna's visitors are tourists. Although," he added, surveying the straggling village of whitewashed, thatch-covered houses, "it appears that none have come today, which is fortunate for us. We have the choice of being married by a fisherman, a smuggler, a joiner, a tobacconist, or the traditional blacksmith, and he will ask whether you have come here willingly.''

"I do. I have,'' she said breathlessly, her lips still throbbing in reaction to his kiss.

"Then take off the ring you are wearing now, because I am going to replace it with another very soon.''

A few minutes later, Nerissa stood in a dimly lit room facing a shabby individual who wore a coat liberally flecked with ash from his pipe and appeared to represent several of the professions Nick had named. Although he declared he was a professional "joiner,'' the local slang for a priest, the walls of his humble cottage were lined with the jars of tobacco and snuff he offered for sale. A liberal stock of whiskey barrels confirmed Nerissa's suspicion that he supplemented his income by smuggling the goods of some local, unlicensed distillery, but she saw nothing to indicate that he was a blacksmith, though he did conduct the ceremony over an anvil, as required by custom.

Six guineas was the price demanded of the groom, who readily paid the sum. "Ye must treat my friends to a glass of whiskey apiece,'' the Scotsman said, nodding in the direction of the witnesses he had called in. "And if ye've brought a ring, give it to the lady.'' When Nick had done this, he barked, "What's yer name?''

"Dominic Sebastian Charles Blythe.''

"A reet mouthful, that. Lassie?''

"Nerissa Rosalind Newby,'' she replied.

"Where d'ye bide?''

"London,'' Nick answered.

In the periphery of her vision, Nerissa saw a coin change hands; obviously it was the habit of the witnesses to wager on the outcome of that question.

"Are ye both single folk?''

"We are,'' said Nick.

Turning to Nerissa, the old man asked if she had come of her own free will and accord, and she replied in the affirmative. There was a brief pause in the proceedings while he quaffed the contents of his tankard. Then, "D'ye take this woman to be your lawful wedded wife, forsaking all others, and keep to her as long as ye both shall live?"

"I will," said Nick.

After Nerissa had answered the same question, the Scotsman asked her for the ring, which he then transferred to her bridegroom, who placed it on her finger. Nick repeated the vow, saying, "With this ring I thee wed, with my body I thee worship, with all my goods I thee endow, in the name of the Father, Son, and Holy Ghost, amen."

"Now, lassie, ye must say 'What God joins together, let no man put asunder.'" The words were hardly out of Nerissa's mouth when the old man said hurriedly, "Forasmuch as this man and this woman have come together by giving and receiving a ring, I therefore declare them to be man and wife before God and these witnesses."

When all was done, a dazed Mrs. Blythe asked, "Aren't we supposed to sign a register?"

"Only if ye want to."

She was about to insist upon it, but Nick suggested that they dispense with the formality. She nodded, for to leave behind any proof of their belated nuptials might result in discovery and embarrassment. And Nick, being a fugitive from the law, could not run the risk of signing his true name.

He bought their well-wishers the promised dram and purchased some pipe tobacco for himself from the Scotsman, and when Nerissa followed him out of the cramped dark house, she was surprised to find she felt no different than she had upon entering it.

"Being wed at Gretna is not nearly as romantic a

procedure as one is led to expect,'' he commented. ''I hope you aren't disappointed?'' Nerissa, thoroughly disoriented from all that had occurred in so short a time, shook her head and let him lead her back to the waiting chaise. Their postboy, none the wiser, climbed into his saddle and pointed the horses to the south.

As the carriage retraced its earlier path, Nerissa inspected the gold band Nick had placed on her finger; it was chased with a delicate pattern of hearts and flowers. There was an inscription, too. ''Love me and leave me not,'' she read aloud. ''Why, it's the same motto from Nerissa's ring in *The Merchant of Venice!*''

''A jeweller in Carlisle engraved it,'' Nick told her. ''I had intended to give it to you at Christmas, but I decided to put it to a better use.'' His voice was pitched very low as he said, ''I do not demand your love, Nerissa, it may yet be too soon for that. But at least I need no longer fear you will leave me.''

The tide of Nerissa's joy ebbed. Had he married her only for the sake of convenience, because he could not get her into his bed any other way? She banished this thought at once, and tried to look on the bright side— she was wed to a man she loved beyond reason, and furthermore, she could now claim her inheritance, although by law it belonged to her husband. Who, she suddenly recalled, was entirely oblivious to her prospects.

Nick, whose watchful eyes were fixed upon her troubled face, said quietly, ''I hope you aren't regretting this step.''

''Oh, no, it's only that I—'' She broke off, uncertain about how to proceed. At last she plucked up her courage and said boldly, ''Now that I am your wife, there is something I ought to tell you, Nick. It wasn't important before, but you do deserve to know the truth about me.''

She had no way of knowing that this tentative pre-
amble was exactly what he had been dreading, and
although it was not unexpected, it was most definitely
unwelcome. Nick did not want to begin his married
life by listening to his bride confess her liaison with
another man. It would be kinder, perhaps, to tell her
that he already knew about the child, but he couldn't
bring himself to do it.

Peering up at him, she said, "I've never discussed
this—everyone knew it, you see, which makes this a
trifle difficult. I suppose I should just say it straight
out and be done." She took a breath, then blurted,
"I'm an heiress. My father's estate was considerable,
and he left the whole to me—it has been administered
by my trustees, but their power expires upon my marriage, and would have done so on my twenty-fifth
birthday had I remained unwed. The principal is in-
vested in Consols—the three percent consolidated an-
nuities. And I have India stock, and Bank stock as
well. But the larger part of the income derives from
the ships—when Papa sold them, he retained part interest. He was very successful in his business ven-
tures," she said with more than a trace of pride, "and
I believe I may have as much as half a million pounds,
though I've never known for sure. But he told me once
that I would be dowered with one-tenth of his fortune,
and my portion alone is fifty thousand."

Yes, Nick thought bitterly, it would take that much
money to buy a husband for a wayward daughter, heiress though she might be, and obviously Captain Newby
had known it.

Nerissa bit her lower lip in consternation. "You
don't appear to be much pleased."

"I am not a mercenary man," he told her, more
harshly than he had intended.

"I never meant to suggest that you were," she replied calmly, but he could read the pain in her eyes.

His expression softened. Gently he drew her head down to rest upon his shoulder and said, "Today I have gained something of greater value to me than mere money, Nerissa, and I am content."

Within the hour the carriage swung into the drive leading to the farmhouse, and he smiled down at his silent companion. "Home at last."

"Just in time for tea," she murmured prosaically.

"A pity we won't be able to enjoy it in privacy," Nick commented. "It appears we have company."

Nerissa lifted her head and saw that a mud-splattered chaise stood in the yard. "Not the Bow Street Runner?"

"Travelling post? I doubt that very much," her husband replied. "I hope it's not the Runner—surely he wouldn't intrude upon our *second* wedding night!" He pinched her rosy cheek and laughed as if he hadn't a care in the world.

Upon entering the hall they found a trunk and a bandbox, and the parlour was occupied by a short, dark-haired lady. Nerissa paused on the threshold, watching as Nick swept the stranger into an embrace that nearly lifted her from her tiny feet. "Why didn't you warn me that you meant to come north?" he asked when he released the lady, who smoothed her chignon with one dimpled hand and glanced uncertainly at Nerissa. "Come and meet Mrs. Durham," he invited her, before turning back to the lady. "What brings you here, Cat?"

"I had to see for myself how you were faring," she told him.

Nick draped a careless arm around his bride's shoulders and said merrily, "Very well indeed. Since you and I last met, this lady has honoured me with her hand in marriage. And she will be glad of your company, for I am kept busy all the day long—I am no longer the idle fellow you once knew."

He silently blessed his wife when she supported him, saying easily, "Mrs. Durham, I am most happy to make your acquaintance, and I hope you are able to make a long stay. I'm sure the two of you have much to discuss, so if you'll excuse me, I'll tell Alec to carry our guest's trunk to the spare bedchamber and order some tea brought in."

After closing the door behind her, Nick turned to Cat, his expression one of comical dismay. "I hardly know where to begin."

"You said nothing in your letter about being wed!"

He placed a warning finger over his lips, and said softly, "I wasn't, not until two hours ago. We've just returned from Gretna, the only place where the deed could be accomplished with ease, and in complete secrecy." He crossed to the fireplace to take his clay pipe from its rack on the hearth. "Do you mind?" Cat shook her head, so he drew his newly filled tobacco pouch from his coat pocket.

"Lady Blythe is very beautiful," she commented as he tipped some of the mixture into the clay bowl.

"Isn't she? But you must take care not to expose me, Cat, for despite our having lived together as man and wife—or very nearly—all this while, Nerissa is quite unaware that I'm anything other than plain Mr. Blythe. I dispensed with my title many weeks ago, and it was better that she believe in my alias implicitly."

"Surely you mean to tell her the truth," Cat interjected. "I accept that it might have been more prudent to conceal your identity when there was some danger of discovery, but now—"

"No," he said firmly. "She'll need time enough to grow accustomed to our marriage. I can't burden her with the fact of my being a nobleman just yet."

With a sigh of resignation, she replied, "Oh, very well, I suppose you know best. But trust me, for I speak as a woman, you had better tell her soon, or you'll rue it.'' Reaching for her fringed reticule, she said, ''I've brought your thousand pounds in the form of a draft drawn upon my bank in St. Albans.''

''Your arrival is most timely, for my resources are sadly diminished. Living isn't cheap, not even in this remote part of the world, and I had no very clear notion what it would cost to set up housekeeping. My word, the things I've had to purchase—furniture and a carriage, and milk cows and a horse, and a host of other things.''

''Which you've always taken for granted, spoiled fellow that you are—or were,'' Cat said, dimpling up at him.

''Was I? Well, those days are long gone.'' Nick sat down in his usual chair and stretched his legs out comfortably. ''Nerissa, I've lately learned, is an extremely wealthy woman in her own right. I could probably purchase half of this shire with her dowry, but I don't know when I'll have access to her funds. Her trustees won't be pleased to learn that she's Lady Blythe, although they cannot withhold her inheritance. My marriage will have to be made public, for I may have to remain here for a very long time, and I can't have the legitimacy of any issue open to question. Tomorrow I will go to Carlisle to have a new will drawn up. I'll have to reveal my legal name, but it's a risk I'm obliged to take—I must make provision for my wife. Fortunately there's no entail on Blythe; I can leave it to her outright. Ram is heir to the title until I have a son to follow me, but—''

''Oh, how *could* I be so forgetful!'' Cat interrupted. ''I meant to tell you the moment you walked in the door, and here we sit talking of money and wills and such! Nick, he visited me!''

''Who?''

''Your cousin, the viscount—and I was never so amazed in my life, or so frightened!''

Nick lifted his brows. "Did he offer you *carte blanche?*"

"Don't be absurd, of course he didn't. But I'd almost rather he had, for then I should have known what to say!" she said fiercely. In a calmer voice she explained, "He came to St. Albans last week, and wanted to know if I could tell him where you're hiding. Finding you appeared to be a matter of some urgency to him."

Nick puffed thoughtfully on his pipe. "What did you say?"

"Very little. He did most of the talking, and I didn't understand the half of it. He kept saying he hoped you hadn't fled the country, because it would hurt your case."

"*What* case?" he asked wryly. "I have none, as he must surely know."

"I confess, he made me feel very ill at ease. I cannot but wonder if he intends some sort of mischief."

But Nick cared very little about his cousin's reasons for visiting Cat, and he listened to the rest of her tale with only half an ear. As glad as he was to see a familiar face, her arrival on the scene would prevent him from pursuing that greater intimacy he hoped to achieve with Nerissa. He had wanted her, he had wed her, and yet, he reflected, he had not really won her trust if she was still unwilling and unable to reveal the fact of her son's existence. Luring her to his bed had long been his goal, but as soon as he got her there he would face the inevitable explanation of why she was no virgin.

At least, he told himself as he idly blew a perfect ring of smoke, the drawing up of his new will and the negotiations for the purchase of Arcadia Farm would serve as much-needed distractions. Although nothing could prevent him from regretting his present inability to claim the lady who was now his wife.

9

ALTHOUGH NERISSA, WHO spent her wedding night alone, was perplexed by her bridegroom's failure to come to her, it encouraged her to hope that he'd had other reasons for marrying her apart from the obvious one. At breakfast the next morning, it almost seemed as if she had dreamed the event of the previous day, for Nick did not allude to the change in their circumstances. When he explained that last night he and Mrs. Durham had sat up talking till the candles guttered, she wasn't sure whether he intended it as an explanation of why he had not sought her bed, or an excuse. And by the time he rose from the table, saying he must hasten to Carlisle, it was even more clear to her that the hurried ceremony at Gretna had effected no material alteration in the structure of their life at Arcadia.

Her first official task as a married lady was taking care of the household mending she had neglected the day before. She was working in the parlour when Sally Willis came to announce that Mrs. Durham was awake but still abed. "I've just taken a tray up," said the maid, "and she bade me give you good morning and say she'd be downstairs soon. Oh, and Mrs. McNab is wanting to know if she should dress some of the fowls master killed t'other day."

Frowning at a tiny, jagged rent in the sleeve of her husband's shirt, Nerissa said, "We'll have them for our dinner. I'll make a syllabub—you must remember to reserve some of the new milk for it.''

''Aye,'' Sally said absently, her attention caught by something in the window. Wringing her apron, she reported, ''There's a gentleman riding up the drive, wearing shiny boots and a tall hat, like the town-folk.''

Nerissa laid Nick's shirt across the arm of the sofa and went to see. The man, a stranger to her, was exactly as Sally had described him, and his fashionable garb stilled her instant fear that he might be a Bow Street Runner. When he dismounted, he carelessly tossed a coin to Alec, who had darted out of the stable yard to take charge of the horse. ''Answer the door,'' Nerissa told Sally over the insistent hammering of the knocker, ''and if he wishes to speak to Mr. Blythe or me, you must remember to ask for his card.''

''What will I do with it, mistress?'' the country-bred girl asked dubiously.

''Bring it to me,'' Nerissa instructed her. ''Don't worry, it's what he will expect.''

But the maid returned empty-handed, saying breathlessly, ''He's got no cards with him, but he told me he's a *lord!* Am I to let him in?''

Nerissa nodded, thinking that he must be one of the Howards from Castle Corby, for there was no other noble family in the neighbourhood.

When he stepped into her parlour, she realised that he was not as impressive a figure as he had seemed on horseback; though his riding clothes fit well and his boots were highly polished, he was no taller than she, and squarely built. He removed his hat, revealing close-cropped brown hair with tawny streaks in it. ''Is this Arcadia Farm?'' he asked, and she affirmed it with a nod. ''I'm Cavender—Lord Cavender. Dominic must have mentioned me.''

''I'm afraid he didn't,'' she said apologetically.

This appeared to amuse him. ''I daresay old Nick

didn't want to bore so charming a creature by reciting the dull particulars of his family relationships.'' His brown eyes raked her from head to toe, pausing at her bosom in a way that caused her cheeks to flame.

She was quick to clarify the precise nature of her connexion to Nick by saying, with quiet dignity, "Mr. Blythe and I were but lately married, my lord, so I still have much to learn about him." She expected him to leave off staring at her in that rude fashion, but his leer grew even more pronounced.

"*Mr.* Blythe, is it now?" Lord Cavender drawled. "Well, if you do not mind, I shall await his return, but I won't trouble you for anything more than a glass of wine. Though I confess I'm sore tempted." Nerissa glared at him, and he gave a sharp, derisive laugh. "Ah, but the game is up, my beauty—I cannot be bamboozled. If Nick chooses to pass his doxy off as his wife, it's all the same to me. Although if he wanted you to be completely convincing, he ought to have given you leave to make use of his title. Mayn't I call you '*Lady* Blythe'?"

He was drunk, Nerissa thought frantically, or demented. She couldn't decide which would be worse. It was no wonder Nick had failed to tell her about this relation, for nobleman or not he must be a great embarrassment to the Blythe family. Stiffly she said, "I fail to comprehend your jest, my lord."

"Did he not even bother telling you he's a baron? How very remiss of him, to be sure." Lord Cavender moved closer to her, and tipped his head to one side. "D'you come from these parts? What luck for old Nick, finding so fine an armful to warm his bed in the cold north."

There was a startled gasp from the doorway. Nerissa and her visitor turned to see Cat Durham, who cried, "For shame, Lord Cavender! You must not say such things to this lady!"

"Lady, my eye!"

"Mrs. Durham," said Nerissa faintly, as she eyed the unrepentant viscount, "do you know this gentleman?"

"Enlighten the wench, Cat. Tell her who I am. Clearly she thinks me something less than sane, and I gather you two ladybirds speak the same language."

"I will not bandy insults with your lordship," was Cat's quelling reply. "When Lord Blythe returns—" She hesitated, realising what she had just said.

"Never mind," Lord Cavender laughed. "I've already revealed the terrible truth about her so-called husband, the fictitious Mr. Blythe."

Through lips that were stiff and dry with shock, Nerissa whispered, "Is it true, then, what he said about Nick being a baron—it was *not* a jest?" And when Cat bowed her head in confirmation, the room spun sickeningly around her. She tried to focus on the faces of the lady and gentleman, one so anxious and concerned, the other blatantly mocking, and struggled to gather her scattered wits together. The effort proved to be beyond her.

"You are amazed," Cat said sympathetically, "and well you should be. I told Nick, I warned him how it would be, but he is so stubborn."

"It is not your fault. I think," Nerissa heard herself say, "that I must excuse myself. I suddenly feel the need to—to lie down."

She was halfway up the stairs when Lord Cavender said, in a carrying voice, "D'you suppose she meant that for an invitation, Cat? Ought I to follow her?"

But his malice could not wound her; she was too numb.

Ramsey Blythe, tense and out of temper, twirled the long stem of a wine glass between his fingers. He had the parlour to himself now—first Nick's bold-faced beauty had disappeared, and then Cat Durham, after waving her little paws and mewling at him, had stalked off. Eventually he had induced the shy little maidservant to bring him some wine, quizzing her about where her master had gone. To Carlisle, she had replied, and his glowering reception of this news sent her scurrying from the room. The irony of it was most irritating: Ramsey had just come from that city, riding over one of the worst roads he had encountered during the whole of the past week.

He could have come here sooner, but he had preferred to remain in London, enjoying his new riches and the pleasures they provided. Then his benefactor had demanded his instant attendance at the Swanborough hunt. Fearful of having offended Mr. Meriden, Ramsey had sent his horses ahead to Leicestershire and travelled there himself a few days later, but without expecting Lady Miranda Peverel to live up to the accolades the old nabob had heaped upon her unsuspecting head. To his amazement and delight, he discovered her to be everything his matchmaking relative had promised, and more. Only seventeen years old, with black hair and deep blue eyes that proclaimed her Marchant blood, she was as lovely as she could be, the embodiment of grace and charm—all in all, a piece of perfection. After a single day of basking in her sweet smiles, he made up his mind to wed her, only to have his uncle remind him that he had not yet made a push to find Lord Blythe, as he had promised.

Cat Durham's extreme nervousness at the time of his visit to her house had alerted him that she knew a great deal about his cousin's whereabouts. One of her servants had let it slip that she was planning a journey, and when she left St. Albans early the next day, he had travelled in her wake, risking discovery by putting up at the same middling inns along the way in order that his postboy, a born spy, could glean information from hers. Upon reaching Carlisle he lost track of her, but sheer luck led him to the Blue Bell in Scotch Street. When he asked the proprietor if a gentleman by the name of Blythe lived within the radius of the great border city, the man replied that Mr. Blythe and his lady had stayed at the inn before taking up residence at Arcadia near Wetheral.

There would be a lady, of course, Ramsey thought as he shifted a sewing basket aside so he might sit down on the sofa. Sipping his wine, he marvelled that even in this remote place his cousin had managed to fill his cellar with decent vintage and his bed with a lovely female. Count on Nick to land on his feet, for rustic though his hideaway turned out to be, it was a surprisingly snug one. The land surrounding the vast stone pile was scrubby and sparse, useless for hunting and fit for nothing but sheep, but those it seemed to support by the hundreds.

He glanced impatiently at the clock. What the devil was keeping Dominic in Carlisle all this time? And a full hour went by before he had the opportunity to put that question to his cousin, who, Ramsey noted with resentment, didn't seem at all surprised to see him.

"It was imperative that I visit an attorney," the baron said as he pulled off his driving gloves. "But my landlord, with whom I also had business, has been called away to Dumfries, so I'm back much sooner than I meant to be."

Ramsey had expected—even hoped—to find Dominic had changed, but saw no sign that he was bowed by his misfortune. His handshake was firm, his carriage as self-assured as ever, and the grey eyes remained bright with good humour even when Ramsey said cuttingly, "Are there no barbers in the north of England? What a shaggy fellow you have become!"

Dominic reached up to shove his ragged hair out of his eyes and retorted, "And you are looking more spruce than I remember. Cat said you'd be nosing 'round and asking questions, so I knew you were on my scent, but I never guessed you would run me to ground. Well, now that you're here, you must let me show you the farm.'' He forestalled Ramsey's intended objection by saying in a subdued voice, ''I think we had better postpone any discussion until there is no danger of our being overheard, don't you?''

During a very thorough tour of the pigsties and the dairy, Ramsey feigned a polite interest, bobbing his head sagely as Dominic enthused over the hardiness of the herdwick sheep swarming on the fells and dales. He cared nothing for farming, only for horses, and it almost broke his heart when he saw the sole occupant of the stables, a placid grey mare that pulled the humble gig and carried his cousin to the village or the town. He dutifully admired the new chaise, but when he heard that Nick intended to buy carriage horses, he couldn't help saying disparagingly, ''I doubt you'll find anything to suit you in *this* neighbourhood. Now where are we bound?''

''There's an excellent view of the country from the top of the hill,'' Dominic said as he vaulted over a low stone wall, and Ramsey could do nothing but follow him. ''Justin is well, I trust?''

''I seldom see him now he has become Lord Elston's boon companion.''

''You've never liked Damon very much, have you? Or me,'' Dominic added grimly, but without rancour. ''Which is why I have to wonder at your taking the trouble to visit me—a taxing and expensive journey.''

Now the time had come for Ramsey to state his business. ''I've come here in the hope of persuading you to return to London.''

''And risk having my neck stretched with a silken rope? Your concern for my welfare is most endearing, coz.''

"It's concern that brings me here," Ramsey puffed, trying to keep pace with his taller cousin's stride. "Dominic, the longer you remain in hiding, the harder it will be to convince the world of your innocence."

"I doubt it can ever be convinced. Haven't you looked into a newspaper lately?"

Ramsey gave a dismissive shrug. "I've spent most of the past two months in town, and I assure you that very few people—important people—have been swayed by the lies that have been printed."

"You relieve my mind considerably," Dominic said dryly. "As for the other million or so souls in London, do you suppose I care nothing for what they must think?"

"Popular opinion will change as soon as you've been cleared of the murder charge," Ramsey was quick to point out. "But for that to happen, you must first come forward to defend yourself, or at the very least, seek to have the coroner's verdict overturned. We'll find a pliant magistrate to do it for us, and a year from now hardly anyone will remember that you killed a man."

They halted at the crest of the hill, beneath a spreading oak with gold-brown leaves valiantly clinging to its branches. Dominic turned to Ramsey and said, "I have no intention of leaving this place. I won't say I never will," he went on thoughtfully, "for I'd like to be able to return to Blythe—someday." Leaning against the trunk of the tree, he crossed his arms over his chest. "We've never had much in common, Ram, yet I think I know how you must have felt upon giving up Cavender Chase. But at least you have the freedom, if not the funds, to live there."

"It happens that I do have expectations of reclaiming my estate, for my Uncle Isaac Meriden has designated me his heir."

Dominic, who had been stirring the ground with the toe of his boot, looked up. "The nabob?"

"He has given me a generous allowance, and even put me in the way of a suitable marriage," Ramsey answered. His new sense of superiority was too sweet, too heady to keep him from puffing off his own good fortune to the very man whose life he had ruined. But deep down, he despised himself for it.

"Are you seriously thinking of matrimony? You are hardly the stuff good husbands are made of, Ram."

This criticism prompted him to retaliate by saying, "And what of you? That ramshackle house down there is filled to the rafters with females—and one of them your own father's fancy-piece!"

"You're sadly off the mark if you think there's anything shameful about my relationship with Mrs. Durham," his cousin replied with a maddening smile.

"And what about the other one?" Ramsey taunted him. "Oh, yes, I've seen her. A showy bit of goods, not in your usual style at all—she casts your little Ellen into the shade. Have you finally outgrown your deplorable fancy for plain, simple fare?"

His voice dangerously quiet, Dominic said, "Mark me well, Ram, I will not permit you to attach such slanders to Lady Blythe."

"You don't mean to say you've actually *married* that doxy?" Perceiving that his cousin's face was rigid with anger, Ramsey took a nervous, backward step. "I do earnestly beg your pardon, if she is indeed your wife."

"Surely Nerissa told you we are wed?"

"She tried," Ramsey admitted, avoiding his eye.

"And you didn't believe her?" There was a brief silence. "Well, I'll smooth things over somehow—fortunately my bride has a sense of humour. But you are very much mistaken in thinking Nerissa was my mistress, for she has only ever been my wife."

Feeling his way cautiously, Ramsey said, "You can't have known her very long."

"We met soon after I left London. And even if that

damned duel hadn't placed me in her path, I'd have found her—I like to think so, anyway. We were made for each other.''

Ramsey had never heard that warm note in the rough, uneven voice; his lip curled derisively. At the same time, he was conscious of the stirrings of the same envy he'd always felt for his cousin. In an attempt to bolster his own ego, he conjured up the image of Lady Mira—sister to an earl, niece to a duke, and superior to Lady Blythe in every way. "What is her ladyship's family?" he asked loftily.

"Her name was Newby. Her father, although something of an original, was a gentleman, although you may not believe that when I add that his fortune derived from trade.''

Suddenly it occurred to Ramsey that he might use Dominic's strong feelings to his own advantage. He tried for a concerned, reasonable tone as he asked, "Is it quite fair to your lovely lady, keeping her hidden away in this northern fastness? She is a baroness, she deserves to take her rightful place in society.''

"You are sadly off the mark if you think Nerissa pines for London and high life. She was brought up to value other things besides the shallow pursuits our tonnish friends delight in.'' Dominic added quietly, "Her life has not been easy of late, and I will not make her uncomfortable by stirring up my own sad scandal.''

"You are a fool, Nick,'' Ramsey spat, "and your refusal to face the charges against you makes me wonder if you are not also a coward.''

Head high, his eyes as hard as agates, Dominic said, "Call me a murderer as well, then, and begone. Your insults mean nothing to me, Ram. This may be difficult to understand, but I've never been happier in my life, and this northern fastness, as you call it, is very much my home now. Here I will remain, with or without your approval.''

Ramsey protested, but to no avail; his cousin was adamant in his refusal to leave Cumberland.

By the time he rode away from Arcadia Farm, he was blazingly angry. Dominic was stupid, stubborn, selfish, and lost to all consideration of how his continued exile went against the interests of the Blythe family. And it was particularly galling that he should regard himself as a happy man, when to his own relations and to the majority of his acquaintance he was an object of pity. But Ramsey's defeat went far beyond his failure to convince Lord Blythe to return to London, for he had not yet relieved himself of that tortuous, gnawing sense of culpability for his act of spite on that long-ago October night. He was responsible for the death of one man and the ruin of another, and whatever happened, he knew he would carry that burden to his grave.

After waving Ramsey off, Dominic returned to the house, trying to think of some way to make Nerissa laugh at his cousin's foolish misapprehension about her status in his household. The door to her bedchamber was closed, so he knocked, calling her name. There was a muffled, indistinguishable reply, and he turned the handle.

Nerissa reclined on the low wooden chest covered with a goosedown bolster which she'd fashioned into a windowseat and to which she often repaired with one of her books. But she was not reading. In a dead and distant voice she said, "My lord?"

If she had thrown something at him, or wept, or raged, he might have known how to respond, but her complete inaction left him at a loss. "I can explain," he began, wondering if she would give him the chance. "You mustn't think I didn't trust you enough to tell you, for I never doubted your loyalty, I swear. But you were better off not knowing the truth about me—if I'd been captured, taken up by the Runner, you would have been questioned, too. So long as you remained ignorant of my identity, no real harm could come to you. I was planning to tell you, and Cat warned me I shouldn't put it off, but I wanted you to have time to adjust to the marriage. And part of my reluctance was because of the way you reacted when you learned my name is Dominic and not Nicholas.''

"It hardly matters now," she said dully. "I accept that you had your reasons. But I confess, it is unsettling to learn that the man I thought I married yesterday does not even exist. I am wholly unacquainted with Baron Blythe." She tilted her head away from the window and said, "What were all the names you gave when we were wed? There were so *many*."

"Dominic Sebastian Charles Blythe," he repeated.

She tilted her head away from him. "And where is Lord Cavender?"

"He has returned to Carlisle."

"You should have invited him to stay to dinner. Or didn't your lordship think he would sit down at the table with your doxy bride? Of course," she continued on a harsher note, "he must be eager to return to London and tell all of your grand friends about this misalliance."

"You refine too much upon the title, Nerissa," he said with ill-concealed impatience. "I am only the second person to hold it, and my father was ennobled a mere decade ago. What difference if I am a nobleman? It doesn't stop the people in the streets of London from calling me a murderer."

"When you believed me to be naught but a lowly merchant's daughter, you refused to wed me," she said venomously. "And it doesn't require much in the way of the imagination to guess just why you suddenly chose to regularise our liaison. You felt sorry for me, poor, ruined creature that I am—but in case you have forgotten, I lost my reputation before you ever met me. Your sense of obligation must have been especially keen after I revealed that I'm related to a rich and powerful duke, for only then did you bother to rush me to the altar—or rather, to the anvil,'' she amended.

"I had many reasons for marrying you," he said, but she stilled him with a glance.

"Oh, you wanted me in your bed, too—you have always been honest about that. And you must require a legitimate heir to your title and whatever estate you may possess." Nerissa bounded up from her seat and faced him, her body quivering with rage. "Well, I may *be* your wife, but if you lay a finger on me, you will rue it."

"You did not refuse the terms," he shot back. "It takes two to make a marriage."

"Or to unmake one."

Her cold words sent a shiver down his spine. "And are you perchance implying that you would seek to have this union annulled?"

Without quite meeting his eyes, she asked, "Could I?"

It was not exactly the answer he had dreaded, but it was bad enough. "I won't deny that you could make a very convincing case, for I misrepresented myself to you, and the marriage hasn't been consummated. Yet no court, temporal or ecclesiastical, will set you free." On a note of cruel triumph he concluded, "Because, my dear wife—and so you will remain, like it or not— you cannot dissolve a marriage if you are unable to prove that it ever took place."

And with that, he turned and walked out of the room, leaving her to think of him what she would.

=== 10 ===

THE DAIRY, A squat stone building behind the farm-house, was Nerissa's refuge, the one place where she could be alone with her thoughts and yet make herself useful. One chill December morning she was there, and troubled though her mind was, her hand was steady and sure as she propelled the tin skimmer, scraping the thick, yellow cream from the top of the milk pans. With a deft flick of her wrist, she tipped the cream into an earthenware container at her elbow and moved on to the next pan.

She and Dominic had not made up their quarrel, and the opportunities to do so diminished each day as they grew farther and farther apart—and without ever really being together, she thought unhappily. Now that the scales had been lifted from her besotted eyes, she saw quite clearly that their union was nothing more than an act of condescension on his part. However well connected, the reckless daughter of the eccentric Captain Newby was no proper bride for Baron Blythe. Constrained by his sense of duty—and of honour—he had elevated her to a position for which she was un-worthy, and to which she was most ill-suited. For the present he might be willing to overlook her lack of birth and proper upbringing, for he was an outcast, detached and displaced from his privileged, titled cir-cle of friends. But one day he might resume his former mode of life, and although for his sake she would be

glad when that time came, for her own, she dreaded
it.

When she had taken all of the cream from the pans,
she emptied the skimmed milk into a pail, where veg-
etable parings and table scraps would also find their
way before the whole was fed to the pigs at the end of
the day. She rinsed the pans with spring water and
strained the morning's milk into them, covering each
one with a cheesecloth. She was washing her utensils—the skimmer, strainer, and ladle—when the outraged cackle of the geese in the yard warned her that
someone had trespassed upon their territory, and hers.

A moment later, Cat Durham stuck her head into
the dairy to say with satisfaction, "*Here* you are—I've
been looking everywhere! Mrs. McNab is growing impatient and wants to know when she can begin making
her butter. Can I be of assistance?"

"I'm almost finished, but you may dry these wet
things." Nerissa tossed the cloth to Cat.

"You ought to have Sally do that," the other lady
commented as Nerissa swabbed the stone floor with a
mop.

"Mrs. McNab keeps the poor child busy enough in
the kitchen. Besides, a lady ought not to set her servants to any work that she is not prepared to undertake
herself."

"Whoever said so?"

"My Aunt Portia. She was the most compleat
housekeeper."

During the past fortnight, the two ladies had grown
close, and although Nerissa had never expressed it,
she was grateful to Cat for extending her visit. She
kept Dominic well entertained, playing piquet with
him of an evening, or relating the bits of town gossip
which had come her way, and at table she maintained
an even flow of conversation. Nowadays, the only time
he smiled was when Cat made a jest, or told him an

amusing story about some society person he knew. In the rare times when the Blythes found themselves alone together, they spoke scarcely a word, but in Cat's presence they were forced to behave as a couple, however ill-matched they might be.

"Do we go to church tomorrow?" Cat asked, shaking the water from the milk strainer before applying her cloth. "A collection will be taken up for the Trafalgar wounded, and for the widows and orphans of the men who died. And there's to be a great thanksgiving for the victory, by the King's decree."

Never in her life had Nerissa felt less thankful, although naturally she was glad that the French navy was no longer the threat it had been before the great battle. "Yes, I suppose we ought to attend," she replied.

"Nerissa," said Cat, for the two women were now on terms of familiarity. "I am glad of this opportunity to talk to you in private, about something that has been on my mind for many days. I'm afraid I've outworn my welcome at Arcadia—I have imposed upon you and Nick entirely too long."

Nerissa's face was a mirror of dismay. "Cat Durham, if you go away now, I think I shall never forgive you!"

"I must not stay," Cat replied, shaking her head. "Really, I cannot bear to see you and Nick hurting each other this way—your silence, your anger, are breaking my heart as well as both of yours. Can't you forgive him for deceiving you, Nerissa? Not once in all the years I've known him have I seen him so—so miserable."

"It is not only the deception," Nerissa said uncomfortably. "He should never have wed me, Cat. Our marriage was made too hastily, and for all the wrong reasons. I ought not have accepted him, but on the way to Gretna he was so persuasive, he said all the things

I most wanted to hear. He even kissed me.'' She placed her fingers on her lips, then removed them to say, "But he hasn't done it since.''

"Well, how *can* he, when you have not given him the chance?'' Cat pointed out reasonably.

"If he really wanted to, he would not wait for that.''

"Be kind to him,'' Cat pleaded. "He lost his reputation, which is everything to a gentleman, and he had to leave his friends and family and every one of his possessions behind. You could be his comfort now—his helpmeet.''

"I will try to be,'' Nerissa promised. "But it is harder than it was before, because I know he only wanted me as a mistress, not a wife. And now,'' she said softly, to herself, "I am neither.''

For most of the afternoon the skies had been spitting snow, and now that it was December the days were short and darkness fell early. With scant consideration for his own or the mare's safety, Dominic spurred her on to greater speed, impatient to reach the warmth and shelter of the farmhouse. What sort of welcome would he get upon his arrival, he wondered as the horse lunged ahead. Cat, bless her soul, would probably greet him at the door, her face wreathed in smiles to make up for Nerissa's failure to summon up even one.

Where had she gone, that bold, laughing girl who had stolen his heart? He'd entered this marriage with the best of intentions, only to see it fail before it ever had a chance to succeed. Within twenty-four hours of speaking her vows his bride had spoken of an annulment, and he had heard himself state the impossibility with a brutality he never ceased to regret. Not that he expected her to congratulate herself on the match—he might be a nobleman, but he was an exiled one, and known to the world as a murderer.

Seeing her as she had been these past two weeks, so

grave and troubled, he had resolved to remove the stain of scandal from his name. What he would not do for Ramsey, or even himself, he had to do for Nerissa.

Today he had revoked his offer for the farm and had given notice to quit when the term of his lease expired, whereupon Mr. Haslam had proposed a figure that was more in line with what Nick would have willingly paid only a few weeks ago. He had wearied of life on an upland sheep farm, he had said mendaciously, but in the end he had told his landlord a partial truth, that family business required that he return to London.

The more Dominic considered his position, the stronger it seemed to him. He had not murdered Sir Algernon Titus, and at least three others beside himself knew it: Justin, Damon, and Georgiana. If any one of them came forward to verify his claim of innocence, he might well be able to salvage something from the wreck of his reputation. The blot upon the Blythe escutcheon would never be completely erased, but to be able to pick up the threads of his old life, to pass his days at Blythe or in town as he pleased—that would be freedom indeed. Society might not welcome him back with open arms, no doubt people would always whisper about him as soon as his back was turned, but he could, he decided, live with that.

Crouching over the mare's neck to avoid the snow-flakes slanting into his face, he wondered what Nerissa would say when she learned he was leaving her behind. It would not be easy for him, but he really had no choice; he could not thrust her into the nightmare of his own making, not after everything she had endured. As soon as he cleared his name he would send for her—and what a stir she would cause in London, where her dramatic looks would attract notice and comment. And when they wearied of town life, they would retire to the country, to his beloved Blythe, with its green and rolling parkland and fertile hills.

Through the thick veil of snowflakes he could make out the farmhouse, so different from the graceful brick mansion which figured in his thoughts. There was a light shining in the parlour window, and a figure silhouetted there. He guessed it was Cat who was watching for him, but was pleased to discover it was his unclaimed bride, her lovely face so white and strained that he knew she'd been wearing herself out with some household task. Her determination to keep busy was further proof, not that he needed it, of her discontent.

He was glad to see the teapot waiting; he was chilled to the marrow of his bones. While Nerissa poured out his cup, he told her he had called in Abbey Street, although he did not tell her why. "Miss Haslam sends you her warmest greetings, and she hopes you will visit her soon. Did you and Cat have a pleasant day? Where is she?"

"In her room—packing." When he frowned, Nerissa said hastily, "I did beg her to stay, Nick, but she's adamant about returning to St. Albans."

This was worrying; Dominic had counted on his dear friend and only ally to keep Nerissa company during his absence. Thinking aloud, he said, "Well, neither of us will be able to travel south until the weather improves."

Nerissa could not have looked more stricken if he'd slapped her face. "You are going away?"

"To London."

"Oh. Of course." Her hand shook so badly that she had to set down her cup.

"It is time I answered the charges against me—I must try to establish my innocence. You understand that, don't you?" She nodded, and he said gravely, "I don't know what the future holds—I can't be entirely sure that I won't be clapped into prison within the week. And I know I'm leaving with many things unresolved between us. Perhaps I have no right to ask, but will you stay here, and wait until I send for you to join me in town?''

"No," she said firmly, "I will not."

His heart thudded to a standstill. If she had closed her heart and mind against him, he was a lost man.

With her distinctive, sensuous grace, she came to stand before him, and then she gave him back his life by adding, "I will not wait, my lord, because I intend to go to London with you."

During the week it took to make all the necessary arrangements, Nerissa and Cat Durham bustled about the house, making inventories and putting it in order for the next tenant, Miss Maria Haslam, who would take possession as soon as the Blythes vacated.

"My mother is horrified, of course," the spinster said merrily, when she drove out to the farm to bid Nerissa farewell. "But at the age of forty-five, I hope I am not dependent upon her permission when it comes to pleasing myself. I have always loved this old place, and my father, knowing that, has generously let me have it for my very own."

The day of departure dawned. Two chaises had been hired for the journey, and at first light the two ladies climbed into the first one; Lord Blythe and most of the baggage would follow in the other. Cat tried to comfort her despondent companion with the reminder that she left Arcadia in very good hands. As the carriage bumped along the rutted drive beneath the ancient oaks, their branches heavily laden with mistletoe, Nerissa turned her head for a final look at the house that had been her haven and her home.

The southward journey was swift and unattended by any of the discomforts and alarms of her earlier travels with Dominic, and nothing occurred to hinder the progress of the two chaises, which passed town after town in rapid succession. Each night they stopped at a comfortable inn, and over dinner Nerissa and Cat joined in the effort to lift the spirits of their escort, playing cards with him and taking turns reading aloud. But theirs was a forced gaiety, and it dissipated as soon as each lady retired to her private chamber. As she drew nearer to the metropolis, Nerissa's anxiety increased, and not only on Dominic's account. Her life was about to undergo a drastic change, a prospect that was nearly as daunting as his impending ordeal.

No longer would she fill her days with butter-making or furniture polishing. She had no friends in London, except for Laura and Henry Sedgewick and their brood, and in a city so large it would be difficult to discover where they might be living. She would visit Lucy and Samuel, of course—it was pleasant to think that she was now in a position to do something for them. She hoped there might be a vacant cottage on Dominic's Wiltshire estate, similar to the one in Olney. But with her husband's future still so unsettled, it was hardly the time to reveal her tie to the baby, nor the nature of her obligations to him.

Late on the fourth day, the cavalcade drew into Northampton. It was already dark, but Nerissa could make out streets and houses familiar to her. They stopped at the George, which Dominic preferred to the Angel; he was instantly recognised by the landlord, who exhibited no real surprise upon seeing him. That night, as she prepared for bed, Nerissa thought about her old acquaintance Mr. Gudgeon, and Ned the ostler. When she counted the weeks since she and Dominic had met in that very same town, she was surprised that they numbered only ten; it seemed to her that whole years had passed since that October afternoon.

The next morning, while waiting with Cat for the carriages to be readied for the final leg of their journey, she voiced some of her concerns about what the future might hold. "I was not brought up to be the

consort of a nobleman,'' she said, pleating her napkin
nervously. ''Despite my kinship with the Marchants,
I know nothing of how lords and ladies conduct themselves. Oh, I've lived in London, but on the fringes of
fashion, and although I was nominally my father's
hostess, his dinner parties were exclusively male, and
I was more likely to meet artists and philosophers and
men of commerce than aristocrats. Lord Blythe's
friends will think me some kind of adventuress—or
worse.''

''You make too much of the differences between
you,'' Cat said soothingly. ''I doubt that they have
occurred to his lordship.''

''I daresay Lord Cavender pointed them out to
him,'' Nerissa murmured. Whenever she recalled that
gentleman's disdain, she wished she'd had the wit—
and the nerve—to strike his mocking face.

A little while later, when the proprietor of the
George saw his distinguished customers off the premises, he said vaguely, ''Didn't someone tell me that
you had gone abroad, Lord Blythe?''

Dominic laughed mirthlessly, and denied it. ''No,
no, I've been in the north country.''

Shaking his head dolefully, the other man said, ''The
whole world will be London-bound soon enough, to
pay respects to Lord Nelson. He's to be given a grand
state funeral come New Year, and there may be another ere long, for they say poor Mr. Pitt has fallen ill
at Bath. 'Tis sad times for old England, milord, sad
times indeed.''

At St. Albans they paused just long enough to deposit Cat Durham on the doorstep of her brick-fronted
house on Holywell Hill. ''I will be thinking of you
both,'' Cat assured Nerissa, and the two ladies clasped
hands through the open window of the chaise. Glancing up at Dominic, who had climbed out to bid her

good-bye, she said, "If there is anything I can do to help you, my lord, you must be sure to let me know."

"I will—and thank you, Cat."

After signalling to his postilion, he startled Nerissa by climbing into her chaise, taking the place Cat had vacated. They had not been alone together since the day he announced his decision to return to London, and she was painfully conscious of their estrangement. He appeared to be occupied with troubling thoughts of his own, so she gazed out the window, watching for familiar landmarks as they neared London. At the bottom of Barnet Hill they stopped at the Red Lion to have fresh horses put to for the final stage.

Dominic said hoarsely, when the lights of the city began to be visible in the distance, "There have been times when I wondered if I'd ever see London again."

"I, too," she sighed, and he looked over at her.

"Tired? We've not much farther to go, only a few miles now. My servants will have prepared the suite of rooms that belonged to my mother, and I hope you will find them tolerably comfortable."

"I'm sure I shall." Nerissa felt her stomach curl at this reminder that she was now the mistress of a great establishment.

"I doubt the state of Blythe House is desperate enough to warrant that grave face," he said lightly.

Dredging up a smile, she replied, "It's only that my Aunt Portia trained me to manage three or four servants at most, not to organise an entire staff."

When the two carriages halted before Blythe House, one of the many magnificent residences which bounded Grosvenor Square, a trio of liveried footmen came rushing down the steps. One held a branch of candles high, another opened the door of the chaise, while the third took charge of the baggage. "Welcome home, my lord," said the man with the candelabra.

"Thank you, James, we are glad to be here safely, and in good time. Ah, there you are, Drummond."

"My lord, my lady," intoned a black-clad individual as the couple stepped into a high-ceilinged hall flagged with black and white marble. He tendered a folded sheet of paper. "This just arrived for your lordship."

Dominic broke the seal and scanned the few short lines. "Send 'round to the mews and tell Coachman I want the town carriage," he told one of the passing footmen, before turning to Nerissa. "I'm afraid I ought to go—my cousin and Lord Elston are dining together tonight and invite me to join them."

Even as her spirits sank, she said stoically, "I'm sure you are anxious to hear whatever news they may have."

"Drummond will show you to your rooms, and if you desire refreshment, you have only to ask. Do not wait up for me, for I don't know how long I must be gone."

She followed the butler up the graceful, curving staircase, taking note of the allegorical paintings which lined the wall. When he asked if she had brought her personal maid with her, she admitted the truth and hoped it would not diminish her in his eyes. "I have no abigail, but now I am come to town, I mean to engage one."

"Tomorrow I will undertake to visit the registry office, if my lady wishes it, to seek suitable prospects for the position," said Drummond, as he preceded her down a long hallway hung with more paintings.

Her suite was composed of three rooms, a parlour which contained delicate giltwood furnishings and a handsome Aubusson carpet, a bedchamber which was appointed in a similar fashion, and a small dressing room. Nerissa's mood was much improved by the sight of her new domain, with its hangings of pale blue damask and white marble chimneypieces, and her appetite, which had fled the moment the chaise had pulled into Grosvenor Square, suddenly returned. ''Drummond,'' she said with decision, ''will you be so good as to have a bowl of soup sent up to me, and perhaps a piece of fowl, if it is to be had. And I think—no, I am sure that I would like a glass of wine as well.''

The butler inclined his silvered head and murmured respectfully, ''Yes, my lady.''

The moment he was gone, Nerissa collapsed onto the pretty blue sofa in her sitting room. One of her worries could be discarded, because judging by her first attempt, being a great lady wasn't going to be difficult after all.

11

As HE WAS borne eastward along the fog-enshrouded streets, Dominic remembered his last visit to Lincoln's Inn when, as a fugitive, he had taken sanctuary in a district where most persons sought to uphold the law. The carriage stopped in Chancery Lane, and he walked to Southampton Buildings, where he found the narrow house where his cousin lodged. The rickety staircase creaked warningly, and before he reached the landing, Justin flung open the door and called a greeting down to him.

"Come in, come in," the young man invited him. "We had nearly given you up—I've lost my wager with Damon, because I said you'd be too tired from your journey to join us, and here you are. But I'm glad of it—we have so much to tell you!"

"But first," said a cool, familiar voice, "we must congratulate the fellow upon his marriage. You've been a busy man, Blythe."

"I have indeed," Dominic agreed, gripping the hand Lord Elston held out to him.

Justin Blythe shared his apartments with two fellow students at Lincoln's Inn, and in the cramped common room the signs of their habitation were conspicuous: a black woollen gown had been discarded on a chair, casebooks were piled upon the floor, and dustballs had gathered around the skirting boards. "Is she pretty, your bride?'' he asked eagerly, pressing a wine glass upon the new arrival.

"You'll have the opportunity to judge for yourself soon enough.'' Eyeing the table dubiously, Dominic said, "When you bid me to dine with you, I never expected a feast fit for a king!''

"A prodigal, rather,'' said Lord Elston. "It comes from Serle's Coffee House—I ordered the supper and the wine myself, knowing all too well that our ascetic Justin keeps nothing but bread and cheese and ale.''

"That's because they feed us so well at the Lower Table, though not as well as the Benchers!''

The three gentlemen sat down to their meal, which was enlivened by Dominic's description of his flight to Cumberland. The Marquis shook his blonde head in disbelief and said it must have been a great adventure. "Too much of one, at times,'' Dominic said feelingly. "In fact, I met my wife when she shielded me from a Bow Street Runner.''

"A Runner? Are you sure of it? Well, he certainly wasn't chasing *you*, Nick, for to my certain knowledge Bow Street was never set on the case.''

Dominic frowned across the table at his friend. "Yet the papers made it plain that the authorities were seeking me high and low.''

Lord Elston shrugged his shoulders. "Oh, that report was naught but a sop to the common people, who were crying for your blood. No one made the least push to find you—not until Cousin Ram took it into his head to do so. I don't mean to imply that your flight was unnecessary,'' he hastened to say, "for had you remained in town the authorities would have been compelled to act. But your departure saved them the trouble—and the embarrassment—of taking a peer into custody.''

"And now that I've returned, where do I stand with regard to the law?''

Justin replied, "Two magistrates, Blodgett and Crane, of the Marlborough Street court, have already agreed to conduct an enquiry into Sir Algernon's death."

"What are the chances of having the inquest verdict quashed?" Dominic asked.

"That's difficult to say at this stage," was his cousin's evasive reply. "Mr. Peale, for whom I clerk, is willing to discuss the matter with you. I think he will take your case, and you need not worry about having to give evidence, for we'll find some way around that. You did fight a duel, and your opponent did die—these facts cannot be concealed or altered."

"*And* there was a witness," Dominic said, "that damned medical man who told the coroner's jury that I murdered Algy in cold blood. I hardly think he will recant his earlier testimony."

"My effort to locate him has failed," Lord Elston interjected. "And making some enquiries, I ascertained that he has left London, but for reasons that are quite unconnected with your duel. He was in the pay of a band of body-snatchers and worked as a middle man, delivering bodily remains to surgeons and anatomists for dissection. His activities in support of the Resurrection Men had been so *very* sordid that the magistrates are not likely to credit his account of what occurred at Chalk Farm."

Dominic, having eaten his fill of the chops and savoury puddings, leaned back in his chair and said gloomily, "I had hoped this business would be easier, but I see it promises to be very messy."

"I'm afraid so," Lord Elston agreed, "but I don't doubt you possess the resolution to see it through."

"If only Nerissa might be spared . . . I would send her down to Blythe if I weren't reasonably certain that she would refuse to go." Dominic smiled as he recalled his wife's stubborn determination to accompany him to London. "I daresay my leaving town is out of the question?"

"You can ask Mr. Peale," Justin replied, "but you may be sure he will advise against it. I have also consulted with Hill, Serjeant-at-Law of Lincoln's Inn—Serjeant Labyrinth, as we call him. He can cite cases and precedents by the dozen, and although his arguments are complex and generally impossible to follow, he was quite clear about one thing—we must convince the magistrates of the strength of your friendship with Sir Algernon."

"And how," Dominic sighed, "am I to do that, if your Mr. Peale fails to call me as a witness?"

It was Lord Elston who answered his question. "The fair widow possesses a great deal of information that would benefit you, although whether she is willing to reveal it all is yet to be determined."

"Georgiana has already suffered too much—can we not leave her in peace?"

"It's to save your neck, man," the Marquis said testily.

Justin hastened to throw himself into the breach. "The case is not so desperate as all that, Damon."

Dominic turned on his cousin. "Tell me, exactly how desperate *is* it? You've managed to skirt that issue quite neatly, in your lawyer fashion."

"We cannot expect miracles," Justin told him frankly. "If the magistrates bring in a verdict of manslaughter this time, we will have to be satisfied, for in all likelihood you would not be committed to trial. Even though it is a capital offence, the officers of the court are notably lax when it comes to prosecuting duellists, knowing all too well that juries often acquit in such cases."

"Manslaughter," Dominic repeated, and his optimism, faint though it had been, faded away, leaving him prey to a pervading sense of doom.

* * *

At midmorning Nerissa, clad in her Chinese dressing gown, her hair lying loose about her shoulders, ate her customary breakfast of tea and toast in the privacy of her sitting-room. Her husband's entrance took her by surprise and brought the colour rushing into her cheeks; not since their marriage had he seen her *déshabillé,* and she felt unaccountably shy. When he enquired politely if she had slept well, she answered him with a nod, and her eyes followed him as he wandered about the room.

Pausing at the window, he said critically, "These hangings are faded."

Now that she had seen her new surroundings in the light of day, she was inclined to agree, although she said, "By comparison to our former abode, Blythe House is a palace."

"You must have Drummond show you all 'round it—I honestly believe he is prouder of the place than I am, though it was my ancestor who built it. It was known as Cavender House, until Ramsey, ever pressed for funds, sold it to my father, who acquired his fortune in the established way of younger sons. But he married an heiress by design, not by accident, as I did," Dominic said, inspecting one of the china ornaments on the mantel. "Lord Cavender, you will no doubt be glad to know, is safely out of the way, paying court to some young lady in Leicestershire. As he's a hunting man, I'm not surprised he should seek a bride from the shires."

But Nerissa cared nothing for the viscount; she was more interested in what had transpired last night. When she asked him, he shrugged, as if unwilling to discuss it with her.

"Oh, we talked for many hours, Damon, Justin, and I, and managed to come up with a reasonable motive for my damning flight to Cumberland." When he replaced the figurine, he looked over at Nerissa and smiled. "You may save my neck yet again."

She tipped her head to one side. "How so?"

"I've already written the announcement of our marriage and sent it to the papers, and by the end of the week the whole of fashionable London will have heard that we spent a protracted honeymoon viewing the lakes—among other things. That is what we will let them believe, and I beg you to keep silent about the truth of my admittedly unconventional courtship."

Nerissa bit back the retort that there had been no real courtship, for she didn't want to quarrel. She was his wife; it was her duty to support and defend him, and although silence was the only thing he had asked of her, if he required her to perjure herself, she would do it, and gladly.

"I must not linger," he said suddenly. "Mr. Peale, Justin's mentor, is expecting me in his chambers, and after I confer with him I'll be off to the city to present myself to your trustees." After telling her that he would leave the town-carriage at her disposal, he hurried from the room.

Where, Nerissa wondered, did he expect her to go? She had no one to visit except Lucy, and to go rushing to Chelsea hard upon her arrival in London, or to have Samuel brought to Blythe House might well stir up the kind of speculation that had driven her from Olney, and Dominic would inevitably demand an explanation that she was not yet ready to make. From now on she must act prudently. But despite this resolve, she dashed off a letter to Lucy, explaining her new circumstances, and folded it around a ten-pound note. Then she rang for James the footman, and lest he puzzle over her correspondence with someone living in so unfashionable a street as Jews Row she said, with perfect truth, that Lucy Roberts was a former servant.

For someone who was, ostensibly, a lady of leisure,

she spent a busy morning. The butler took her over the house, from garret to cellar, and presented the staff to her with grave formality. The housekeeper, hastily summoned back from a holiday, was taken aback when the new mistress expressed a preference for a tea other than the sort presently served at Blythe House.

"But I've laid in pounds of the stuff, my lady," Mrs. Rogers protested.

"You can serve it at the servants' table," Nerissa said firmly. "I am not particular about most things, but in this I insist upon a change." She was a little afraid she had alienated the woman, but when she supplied the name of a merchant who could be depended upon to carry her favourite blend, the housekeeper regarded her with respect and said she would send someone to make the purchase right away.

Unlike Mrs. Rogers, the gentleman-cook had remained in residence during Lord Blythe's long absence from town. Nerissa's brief encounter with him made her think longingly of Mrs. McNab, for she knew she would not be called upon to help Mr. Anson knead the bread or stir a stew or make a white sauce. And his kitchen, with its row of crockery and collection of gleaming pots and pans, was quite as intimidating as the chef himself.

To her surprise, Drummond's visit to the registry office turned up two excellent candidates for the position of lady's maid. The first of these was a woman of mature years with excellent credentials, but Nerissa feared she might be inclined to despise her mistress's ignorance. And therefore, quite unknowingly, she endeared herself to the footmen in her husband's employ by engaging a young, pretty, buxom lass named Rose.

She didn't need an abigail to point out the sad fact that her wardrobe required attention. Few of the gowns that had been made up for her marriage to Andrew Hudgins were suited to her new estate, so she dis-

patched the ubiquitous James to the nearest bookseller's shop to procure a selection of the latest fashion
journals. After poring over them and making a list of
things she required, she went to the library. Its many
glass-fronted bookcases were filled with tempting volumes, and she was turning the musty pages of a
sixteenth-century florilegium when Dominic found
her.

"I should have known you would find your way into
this room," he commented. "Have you spent the entire day studying my shelves?"

"Oh, no. I managed to restrain myself till now,"
she laughed. "Is this your private retreat?"

"It is, but I am perfectly willing to share it. What
have you found there?" She carried her book over to
him, and after a brief examination he handed it back
to her. "A fine specimen—I'm forever finding treasures I never knew about. Sometimes I make the mistake of removing them to Blythe, which has another
fine collection, so the existing inventory is rather less
than completely accurate. I'll try to find a copy of it
for you, if you like."

"I would." Curious to know how much of her
dowry would be reserved as a jointure, or whether he
would make some settlement upon her, she asked,
"How did you prosper at your meeting with my trustees? Did you persuade Mr. Halpern and Mr. Rose to
release my fortune into your hands?"

He had crossed to the knee-hole desk at the far end
of the room, and was gathering together some of the
many papers strewn across it. "Everything is all arranged—it was a simple, straightforward business.
And the gentlemen, though no longer your trustees,
will continue to administer your father's estate as they
have always done, for their management has been excellent. I keep my own solicitor busy enough with my
affairs. As for the disposition of your house in Olney,

I recommend that you sell it, unless you object for sentimental reasons, in which case a tenant must be found.''

The thought of being tied to Olney in any way made her say hurriedly, ''No, I do not object to selling. What happens to my dowry?''

''It will be tied up in a trust. For the benefit of our children, if our union should be so blessed.''

This was the first time he had ever mentioned the possibility of issue. Nerissa's cheeks burned, and she was relieved when he glanced down at the sheaf of papers in his hand. ''You will have a great deal of correspondence to catch up on,'' she said, and made her escape.

The next morning, in common with the rest of the town, she read the notice of her marriage in a column in the *London Gazette,* which stated that Baron Blythe had wed Nerissa, only daughter of the late Captain Richard Newby, in a private ceremony. Recalling the particulars of that ceremony, its tipsy witnesses and disreputable Gretna priest, she had to smile at the way the conventional phrasing hid the truth. The repercussions were immediate, and for the remainder of the day, footmen clad in the livery of various noble houses delivered congratulatory notes. Nerissa even received one from Laura Sedgewick, now residing in Bloomsbury. But the most notable of all the many well-wishers called in person.

The Duke of Solway's greying hair was thinner than Nerissa remembered and his flesh appeared to be somewhat reduced, but otherwise he was the same Cousin William she had always known. He kissed just as kindly as when she had last seen him, on the occasion of her father's funeral, and she said ruefully, ''How mortifying to think you learned of my marriage in such a way—my only excuse for not calling at Solway House is that I had no idea you were in town. Are you terribly, terribly shocked?''

''Not that, although I admit to some considerable surprise,'' the duke replied, taking a chair. ''Everyone believed Lord Blythe had fled the country, and naturally I had no idea that you and he were at all acquainted. I seem to recall you were planning to marry some neighbour fellow in Buckinghamshire.''

''At one time I was, although it came to naught.''

''Change of heart, eh?''

''I fear that at the time I accepted that proposal I was too distraught to know my own mind,'' she said candidly.

The duke wagged his grey head. ''I quite miss the pleasant little talks Dick and I used to enjoy when I visited him in the Adelphi Terrace.''

''The grand arguments, you mean,'' she said with a roguish smile. ''How is the Duchess?''

''As magnificent as ever—she's coming up to town later this week. My word, but she's having a busy time of it! Our little niece Mira will be making her comeout this spring, and already Her Grace is planning balls and I don't know what. You remember Mira, don't you?''

''Swanborough's daughter is old enough to be presented? I recall that she was a very pretty child.''

''And has grown into a lovely young lady. I suspect that the period of my guardianship will quickly run its course, for I've already had an offer for her hand. Coincidentally, it came from a member of your husband's family. Have you met Lord Cavender?'' She nodded, and he asked, ''And has he told you he's dangling after Mira?''

''Is he? No, the subject never came up. At the time, his lordship was quite ignorant of my connexion to the Marchants and the Peverels, and may still be, for all I know.''

"I confess to you, Nerissa, I like it not. Mira is too young for a man of his years and habits, although to say so to either of them would do more harm than good at this stage."

Seeing how distressed her relative was, she changed the subject. "Tell me about the rest of your family—I am counting on some happy news about the Ladies Ophelia and Imogen—I believe both were in an interesting situation last winter."

"I've two grandsons now," His Grace reported. "But can you credit it, my Gervase still hasn't been caught by any of the lures cast out to him! Edgar has just matriculated at Oxford, for all he's no scholar—his mother has hopes it may steady him." It wasn't long before the duke touched upon Lord Blythe's difficulties, but his words were ones of comfort, not censure. "Your husband is fortunate in having the support of many friends," he said, "and a man who is capable of inspiring such loyalty will surely prevail."

"I pray you may be right, sir, but I know nothing about the particulars of the case. Lord Blythe has not discussed it with me."

"Well, that's because he doesn't want you to worry. Nor should you," he said, pinching her cheek. "Take my advice, and don't encourage him to hide his face, my dear—be sure he goes to his clubs and is seen about town. If you like, you may have use of Her Grace's box at Drury Lane. That little lad who causes so much stir, Master Betty, is playing in *MacBeth* tonight."

The popularity of the youth who had been London's favourite player for the past year was on the wane, but that evening the theatre was crowded with his admirers. Dominic pointed out several famous personalities to Nerissa, among them the Duke and Duchess of Bedford, Lady Holland and Mr. Luttrell, and the Devonshires. The gouty duke and his once-lovely duchess were there in the company of their intimate friend Lady Elizabeth Foster, dressed from head to toe in funereal black out of respect for the departed Nelson. Nerissa derived much amusement from the parade of persons in the box-lobby, and found the audience even more diverting than the actors. During the interval the Marquis of Elston joined the Blythes, and begged to be presented to Nerissa. The extraordinarily handsome young man then embarked upon a light, one-sided flirtation with her, and spun some choice tales about her husband. In the morning, she penned a letter to her noble kinsman, thanking him for the loan of his box.

The following week His Grace's carriage returned to Blythe House, and this time it brought his wife and niece. The Duchess of Solway was, as her fond spouse had said, a magnificent woman; she had passed her fiftieth year, but her hair still retained its rich brown colour and her complexion nearly rivalled that of her companion, a girl of seventeen.

She embraced Nerissa, saying, "My dear, so now you are Lady Blythe! I was astonished when the duke wrote to tell me the news. Mira, my love, make your curtsey to her ladyship."

"Oh *please* do not," Nerissa begged her young cousin. "It makes me feel ancient, and anyway, I've been studying tables of precedence as if my life depended upon it, so I know I should be the one to curtsey to you. The daughter of an earl outranks the wife of a baron!"

Lady Miranda Peverel gave a soft laugh and said in her pretty voice, "Tables of precedence, indeed! And I remember you as being so lively and care-for-nothing."

"Dear me, what a character to live down." Nerissa cast a chagrined glance at the duchess, who, to her surprise, smiled benevolently upon her.

"You were ever like your father in spirit as well as looks," the great lady said. "I do confess that Miss Portia Newby had all my sympathy! I don't doubt that she would be gratified by this match you've made—to think that Dick Newby's daughter snagged Dominic Blythe! Let me tell you, my dear, if your husband had ever shown the least interest in either of my girls, I would have been in transports. Although I must say that Ophelia and Imogen did quite well for themselves. And so, no doubt, will Mira."

Nerissa hardly recognised the poised young beauty as the pale, quiet child she had met years before. Lady Miranda wore a simple white muslin gown that flattered her fragile figure, but Nerissa suspected her appearance of delicacy was deceptive, for she'd been raised among hardy, horse-loving Marchants. The blue eyes were bright with intelligence, and Mira's black hair fell to her slim waist in a cascade of long curls.

The duchess continued, "We have come to invite you and Blythe to attend our Twelfth Night dinner, although I'm afraid it will be less gay this year—we cannot give our usual grand ball afterwards, not with Nelson being interred in the same week. But what say you, will you join us on the sixth of January?"

However honoured Nerissa was to be asked, she could not accept before discussing the matter with Dominic; the magistrates' enquiry would take place the following day.

"Yes, yes," the duchess said briskly when she mentioned this circumstance, "the duke heard the news at his club. He feels—and I agree—that you and Blythe might be glad of something to take your minds off all that unpleasantness. We'll expect to see you, then," she concluded, her tone indicating that as far as she was concerned, the issue was settled. "The progress of the war, that's all anyone cares about these days. The one name on all lips is poor Nelson's—for which you and Blythe must surely be glad. Trafalgar quite eclipsed the scandal of the duel, and now the state funeral will overshadow the inquest.''

Nerissa was prevented from making a reply by her butler, who came to announce the arrival of another caller. "Lord Cavender is here, my lady, and is wishful of speaking with his lordship.''

"Oh, dear." The words slipped out before Nerissa realised it, and she strove to cover this lapse by adding swiftly, "I mean, how unfortunate that Lord Blythe has already gone out. Drummond, please inform Lord Cavender that I will be happy to receive him.''

When the viscount entered the saloon she went to meet him, her head held high—not even the duchess could have outdone Nerissa's show of pride as she welcomed this most unwelcome of visitors. "Good afternoon, my lord," she said graciously, extending her hand.

He bowed over it. "I hope I haven't come at an inconvenient time, Lady Blythe.''

"Not at all," Nerissa said, thinking that this civil encounter was the antithesis of their previous one. "I'm afraid Lord Blythe has gone to one of his clubs with Lord Elston. In the absence of your cousin, I invite you to make do with some of mine—I believe you are acquainted with Her Grace, and Lady Miranda.'' His startled reception of this speech gave her a perverse satisfaction; he was clearly taken aback.

The duchess gave him a long, assessing look. "Lord Cavender, surely you know that her ladyship's father was first cousin to the duke?''

"No, I did not," Ramsey faltered, for he had never guessed that the bold-faced creature he'd met in Cumberland might be a lady born. He hoped she did not hold his past rudeness against him, although if she did, she gave no sign of it. When she invited him to be seated, he took the place nearest Lady Miranda.

"I presume your lordship has come to London in connexion with the inquest," said the duchess, "for certainly you will be much affected by the outcome."

Although Ramsey had suffered a shock upon learning of Lady Blythe's connexion to the Marchants, it was nothing to what he felt now. For one panicked moment, he thought the duchess was hinting—more than hinting—that he was responsible for the baronet's death. He managed to recover his voice, and with a tolerable show of calm he said, "I join with all of my cousin's friends in hoping he may be able to clear his name." Demonstrating a concern for Dominic would surely redound to his credit in Lady Mira's eyes.

It was not long before the duchess and her lovely charge departed, and he took this as his cue to leave as well; Lady Blythe made no attempt to detain him. As he walked away from Grosvenor Square, he wondered if he had been wise to follow his inamorata to town. Perhaps he should have waited until after the New Year—after the magistrates' enquiry into the circumstances surrounding the death of Sir Algernon Titus. But he had been pressured into leaving Leicestershire—not only by his uncle Isaac Meriden, impatient to see him wed to Lady Mira, but also by Justin, who had urged him to support Dominic. His brother so seldom asked anything of him that Ramsey hadn't been able to refuse the request, however disturbed he was by the prospect of attending the hearing. He took some comfort from the fact that nearly three whole months had passed since the party in Clifford Street, so it was quite unlikely that anyone would even remember he'd been present. And as he strolled along Brook Street, his frown of concern was replaced by a smile of triumph.

═══ 12 ═══

CHRISTMAS CAME AND went, but few hearts were made happier by it. Entertainments and celebrations were rare; a pall seemed to lie over the vast metropolis. The British people, already mourning the loss of Lord Nelson, were pitched into deeper gloom upon receiving grim news from the Continent, where the French armies had soundly defeated the Austrian and Russian allies. London's weather was as dismal as the mood of her inhabitants, and in the final week of 1805 an epidemic of influenza attacked the upper reaches of society, keeping many tied to their homes.

On Christmas Day, as Nerissa watched her husband carve the goose, she had to remind herself that this was supposed to be a festive, joyous season. She saw him so rarely that she could have fancied herself single again; their activities kept them apart during the day, and at night he generally dined out. When their paths did cross, he made some comment about her attire, or quizzed her about what book she was presently wearing out her eyes with, and he avoided the subject of the inquest altogether. He made no real effort to break through the seemingly impenetrable barrier of silence that had grown up between them, but what pained her most of all was that this man who had once been so eager to be her lover was a most disinterested husband.

The next day, still feeling low, she supplied her servants with the traditional gift of money, and wrote a falsely cheerful note to her friend into which she placed three shillings as a Boxing Day remembrance for the Sedgewick children. And she was thinking of another child this Christmas, for she had received a smudged missive from Lucy Roberts, containing numerous spelling errors, along with a lock of black hair and a vivid description of the lively young gentleman in her care.

As the old year waned, Nerissa had to put off her visit to Chelsea, for a multitude of callers, mostly female, descended upon Blythe House. All were long-time acquaintances of Dominic's who were eager to pass judgment on his wife—or to see how she was bearing up as the date of the inquest drew near. What these fashionable ladies thought of her Nerissa knew not, nor did she greatly care.

On New Year's Eve, she received a more welcome visitor in Justin Blythe, whose devotion to his cousin had endeared him to her. The young student of law resembled his brother neither in looks nor disposition; his smile was warmer than the viscount's, and his sensitive, fine-boned face more attractive. And although she had initially supposed him to be quiet and grave, she was now able to detect the faint, mischievous light in his brown eyes.

She cast aside her book when he was admitted to the saloon and said in surprise, "Mr. Blythe, I thought you'd gone into the country!"

"I returned this morning, and bring happy news for Nick. But first I had to wish you a happy Christmas, Lady Blythe."

"You really must call me Nerissa," she urged him. "We are cousins by marriage, and I refuse to let you stand upon formality. I have long wanted to thank you for working so tirelessly on my husband's behalf. Mr. Peale is a very capable barrister, I'm sure, but I know you have done much to assist him in constructing the defense.''

Justin said soberly, ''Well, I don't think you'd approve of some of the stratagems by which we hope to convince the magistrates of Nick's innocence. Until now, I never guessed my chosen profession was as much one of stretching the law as upholding it!''

Not until the day of the Duchess of Solway's Twelfth Night dinner did Nerissa pay her long-overdue visit to Chelsea. She left the house in the afternoon, unaccompanied and on foot, walking all the way from Grosvenor Square to a hackney-coach stand in Piccadilly. When the humble conveyance deposited her in Jews Row, she lifted the veil that she had worn over her bonnet to avoid being recognised, and approached Lucy's dwelling.

''Oh, I *do* wish you'd warned me you meant to come!'' said the former laundry-maid as she admitted Nerissa. ''Sam could do with a washing-up—he's that untidy I hate for you to see him!''

''Do you think I care for that?'' Nerissa laughed. ''Where is he?''

''In the kitchen, and a rare mess he is. Come along, miss—my lady, I should say, though 'tis so odd to be calling you so!''

Nerissa followed the young woman down a dim, narrow corridor. ''How is your mother?'' she asked.

''Her joints are something stiff in this weather, but she's in spirits. I'll take you upstairs to see her in a bit—she'll be so pleased.''

The kitchen smelled pleasantly of fresh-baked bread. In the corner a child sat upon the floor, playing with a collection of wooden spoons. He had curly dark hair, and his face was liberally smeared with soot. Turning wide blue eyes upon Nerissa, he clapped his chubby, dirty hands and cried, ''Lady, lady!''

"I don't think he knows me," she said forlornly, as she held out her arms to him. "Come to me, little rogue—you owe me a kiss." The boy regarded her doubtfully, then crawled across the floor to her. "Isn't he walking yet?" she asked Lucy.

"Aye, but he's a lazy lad today. He'll show you his steps when he's more used to you, I'm sure."

Nerissa knelt down and managed to coax the child into her lap. She hugged him close with one arm and used her handkerchief to clean his face. When he tugged at it she let go, and as he examined the lace-edged square of linen curiously, she sighed, "I ought to have brought him a toy."

"Your ladyship mustn't spoil him. Why, I couldn't even bring myself to spend the money you've sent, and put it safe away." Lucy's expressive face wore a troubled frown as she watched Nerissa enjoin Samuel in a game of pat-a-cake. "There's something I left out of my note, being as I don't write so smooth. You won't believe it, my lady, but Will Darcy has returned."

"Has he indeed?" Nerissa exclaimed, looking up. "After all this time? Why, it's been more than two years!"

Lucy's eyes filled, and she wiped them with the corner of her apron. "When he was took from me, I never thought to see him again. And I very nearly didn't. He was serving on the *Ajax,* one of the ships that fought at Trafalgar—in the vanguard, he says, though I'm sure I don't know what that means. During the battle nine men were wounded—Will was one of them—and two of his mates got killed. They put him on a transport, and when it docked at Portsmouth he was given leave to come up to London. Oh, my lady, when I saw him standing there at the door, his arm in a sling, I fainted clean away." The young woman smiled through her tears. "But I think *he* was near to swooning when he met my Sam and learned he was a papa! And he's going to be a husband, now, for the banns have already been cried twice, and on Monday morning we'll be wed. As soon as my mum is well enough for the journey, we'll be going to live at Portsmouth. Will's getting his discharge, and means to work in the shipyards there.''

Nerissa tightened her hold on the child in her lap. She couldn't let Lucy see how painful the joyous tidings were to her, so she strove for a cheerful note when she said, ''How lucky it is that I came here today.''

''Oh, I wouldn't have left Lunnon without bidding your ladyship farewell, not after all you've done for us—and the captain, too, God rest his soul. But you'll not be alone now you've got a husband of your own—and him a lord, no less! And just think, one day you'll have wee ones of your own.''

But would she, Nerissa wondered, as Samuel squirmed out of her embrace and toddled over to his mother.

She tried to imagine a son of hers and Dominic's. He would have dark hair, most likely, and perhaps her husband's fine grey eyes, which dimmed and lightened with his changing moods. Oh, yes, a child would bring great happiness into her life, and especially if it bound her to the man she loved in a way that their beleaguered, strife-ridden marriage had not done. But at whatever the cost to her pride, she would have to take the initiative. For too long she had cowered in the background of Dominic's life, waiting for him to make some conciliatory move. By doing so she had not, she realised, been true to her nature.

It would not be easy. But Nerissa—who had been bold enough to invite a strange gentleman to travel with her, reckless enough to share a room with him, brave enough to marry him—decided then and there that she could find in herself the requisite strength to confess her abiding love for him.

Restless and uneasy, Dominic paced up and down the elegant saloon, clad in full dress for the duchess's party—dark blue tailcoat with silver buttons, silk waistcoat embroidered with silver thread, and satin breeches. With each glance at his timepiece and every chime of the long-case clock, the lines in his face grew deeper and harsher. He had planned to present Nerissa with a selection of his mother's jewelry to wear this night; that pleasure had been soured by her delay. When she had left the house that afternoon she had not taken the town carriage, and that hinted at concealment—of what, he didn't like to think. So he had left the jewel-case on her dressing table with a brief note which contained none of the warm regard that had prompted him to make the gesture.

At half-past seven a hackney-coach pulled up at the door. A moment later Dominic heard Nerissa's voice asking James to pay off the driver, and he hurried into the marble-flagged hall to intercept her.

When she saw him, her smile illuminated her face and she said breathlessly, "I'm late, I know—I rather lost track of time. How *elegant* you look! Poor Rose will have to work miracles upon me." She glanced down at her rumpled pelisse.

It was on the tip of Dominic's tongue to ask where she had been, and why she had returned in a hired carriage instead of her own, but he forced back those questions, fearing the answers. Not once in all the time he'd known her had she looked so gloriously alive, so wondrously happy, confirming his worst suspicions. It broke his heart to see that her clandestine reunion with her son had wrought the kind of transformation that he had hoped to achieve himself.

Within the hour she reappeared, wearing a gown of

dark blue satin cut low at the breast to display a glit-
tering necklace and an abundance of white flesh. The
diamonds in the crescent she wore in her dark hair
shimmered in the light of the chandelier. "Is it too
much?" she asked him. "I wasn't sure what would be
appropriate, for I've never dined at Solway House."

"You do me great credit," he said, going to assist
her with her velvet opera-cloak. As he draped the heavy
garment across her shoulders, his fingers grazed her
warm, bare flesh and she smiled up at him. He ached
to take her in his arms, but the carriage was waiting,
they were expected—and anyway, he wasn't at all sure
that she would welcome his advances. She'd given him
no cause to suspect she was anything other than satisfied with their present arrangement.

Solway House sat at the corner of Mount Street and
Park Lane, across from Hyde Park, and its classical
white stucco facade was particularly impressive when
lit by flambeaux. The great ballroom at the back of
the house was far from being full, for this was but a
family party, but Dominic saw many familiar, friendly
faces.

"I hardly expected to find you in this company, Damon," he said when he came abreast of his friend and
fellow peer. "Most of the guests are related to the
Marchants by blood or marriage."

"Yes, that is precisely why my attendance here is
so very compromising," Lord Elston said. In a mock-
conspiratorial whisper he said, "I am a front-runner
in the stakes for Lady Miranda Peverel—or don't you
read the betting-book at the club?"

"Since when are you hanging out for a wife?"
Dominic accepted a glass of wine from the tray held
out to him by a passing footman.

"I'm not, of course," the younger man confessed.
"But it does one's reputation so much good to be seen
at Solway House—I fancy that's why you were asked

here on the very eve of the inquest. That other aspirant to Lady's Mira's hand, your cousin and mine, was not honoured with an invitation. So if Ramsey accuses me of stealing a march upon him, I beg you to deny it.''

"I will,'' Dominic promised.

"You know, Nick,'' said the marquis, as he looked towards the sofa where Nerissa sat with Lady Miranda Peverel, "if they should clap you in prison, I fear I will not repine with my whole heart. I would dearly love to be the one to console Lady Blythe.''

"That is a singularly uncomforting prospect,'' Dominic said drily.

"I might have guessed that of all of us, you would be the one to settle into a love match. Ram is too selfish, he cares for no one but himself. I'm too much aware of my parents' failures to look upon the institution of marriage as anything but a form of entrapment. And poor young Justin is just that, too poor and too young to think of taking a wife.''

"You know, Damon, whoever advised you to cultivate your innate cynicism did you a great disservice,'' Dominic said, and his friend let his mantle of sophistication slip just long enough to let out a genuine and boyish laugh.

When dinner was announced, the guests made their way into the dining-room in a formal procession which followed the strict rules of precedence. Dominic's partners for the meal were Gervase, the duke's heir, and Lady Miranda Peverel; Nerissa sat on the opposite side of the long table, at His Grace's right hand, with Lord Elston on her other side. She appeared to be well entertained, and so was Dominic. The little Lady Mira, who had not yet been officially presented to society, was proficient in the art of conversation. She deserved a better husband than Ramsey; it was a pity that Damon wasn't going to come up to scratch, but soon there would be plenty of likely fellows hanging about her.

There was much laughter and merriment when the Twelfth Night cake was borne in by a quartet of footmen. The duchess cut it with her own fair hand, and the plates were passed down the table until everyone had one. Lady Miranda's slice contained the pea and the Marquis of Elston found the bean; it was obvious to Dominic that this outcome had been planned ahead of time. The couple were given pinchbeck crowns to wear, and despite his lordship's dismissive remarks about marriage, his blonde head was never very far from Lady Mira's black one, and when she sat down at the pianoforte he gallantly offered to turn the pages of her music. Out of consideration for Lord Nelson's memory, there was no dancing, but card tables were provided for the guests, and Dominic was solicited to partner his host at whist. The duke turned out to be a skilled and indefatigable player, and the game went on until supper was served.

It was several hours past midnight when the Blythes finally returned to Grosvenor Square, and Nerissa, looking delectably sleepy, could not quite hide her yawns. As she and Dominic walked up the staircase she said apologetically, "I know we ought to have come home long ago. Several times I looked into the cardroom to say we might leave, but you and Cousin William were so engrossed in your game that I didn't like to disturb you."

They came to the door of her bedchamber. Dominic wished he might go in with her—he needed so much to be with her, to talk, but her abigail was there, waiting to undress her. So he bade her good-night and continued down the hallway to his own room.

He shrugged out of his evening coat and tugged at his neck-cloth. Before disrobing further he paused to pour a glass of brandy and tossed it off in the hopes

that the fiery liquid would ease him into sleep. His
state of mind and present wakefulness reminded him
of that agonising, endless night before his duel with
Sir Algernon. With the prospect of another one before
him, he reached for the decanter once again, putting
it down with a guilty start when he heard a faint rap
upon his door. He supposed it was his officious valet,
come to pester him, but when he opened it he found
his wife standing in the corridor.

She was still clad in her satin ball gown, but the
jewels were gone. So, too, were her shoes and stock-
ings, and he smiled at the sight of her pink, high-
arched feet. "May I come in?" she asked, and he
stepped back to permit her to enter. As she did, she
glanced about curiously, and he recalled that she had
never seen his room before. "I know it is late, I will
not stay long, but I wanted to talk to you about something. Something very important."

Dominic's mouth suddenly went dry. She had seen
the child; now she was going to ask if she might bring
it into his house. Before he could stop himself he said,
"I know already, Nerissa. I've known ever since the
day we met. Shall I prove to you how far my knowledge goes? He is rising two—or was. He may well
have attained that age by now. Someone named Lucy
looks after him for you, and she, I believe, lives in
Chelsea." As she stared at him, perplexed, he explained, "That afternoon at the Angel when I first saw
you, I overheard everything you said to the young man
who drove you there in the gig. Don't you remember?
When you told him good-bye you gave him a ten-pound
note—for your son."

She drew a long, sobbing breath, and when he
reached out to her, she backed away. "Don't touch
me, don't even speak to me—I must think. Northampton, John—yes, I did give him some money, I remember, and asked him to send it to Lucy. And so you

thought—'' As realisation dawned, she began to tremble all over. "You offered me your protection, you even *married* me, believing me to be unchaste?'' Her hands curled into fists and she pressed them against her mouth.

"I wanted you," he rasped.

"Nick, I have no child.''

"You can't deny his existence, Nerissa.''

"Oh, I don't. But Samuel isn't *my* son, I swear it.''

Dominic's giddiness had nothing to do with the advanced hour, or the brandy. But before fierce exultation completely overwhelmed him, he had to make sure he'd understood her. "You're telling me that you've borne no child—had no lover?''

She smiled wanly. "And all this time I thought I'd left that old scandal behind in Olney. But none of it is true—Sam's mother is Lucy Roberts, who was one of our maids in the Adelphi Terrace. Because she and I were very near in age, we became friends, and it was her habit to confide in me. She had a sweetheart, a coal-heaver, and they planned to be wed in the summer.'' Nerissa paused to take a breath, then asked him, "Do you remember how very active the pressmen were in the spring of 1803?''

"Vaguely—I seem to recall that there were reports of it in the papers.'' He listened closely as she described the events of a Sunday afternoon in May of that year, when a press gang had descended upon Hungerford Stairs by the river to take recruits by force.

"Will Darcy and his mates were on the wharf nearby, and threw coal and bottles at the pressmen to chase them off. In retaliation the gang took Will and one of his friends. Papa had connexions at the Admiralty, and learned that Will was transported to Deptford, where he was taken aboard the *Enterprise*. Later on he was sent to the Nore, where he was assigned to some other ship, but Papa could never discover which one.''

''And your maid was already with child by her young man,'' Dominic said quietly.

''About six weeks later, she came to me. I knew she'd been ill, and I also knew that she and Will had—'' Nerissa broke off and flushed. ''Well, it was no surprise that she was breeding. I went to my father, and he agreed that we couldn't turn her off—he was, as I have told you, exceedingly liberal in his notions and agreed that Lucy should continue in our employ until her lying-in, and after. When the baby was born, I stood as godmother, and even chose his name.'' Nerissa quoted softly, '' 'And the child Samuel grew before the Lord.' That winter, when Papa and I removed from London to Buckinghamshire, Lucy went with us to be our laundress. She lived in a cottage of her own down the lane from our house.''

She sat down upon the edge of the great bed. ''Everyone in the neighbourhood guessed Samuel was baseborn, and that I doted upon him was no secret. The world being what it is, this gave rise to the rumour that he was not Lucy's son at all, but mine. I don't know exactly when the gossip began, but I first learned of it soon after Papa died. I was inclined to scoff, thinking the talk would die down in time, but it didn't. When it touched Andrew's family—he had unmarried sisters—he sent Lucy and the baby away. And that's when I knew that I, too, had to leave.''

''What sort of man was your gentleman, that he would let you go, and in disgrace?'' Dominic asked savagely.

''It was my decision. Lucy's sudden departure, to say nothing of the broken engagement, would have confirmed the gossip rather than refuted it. So I wrote a letter to Laura and closed up my house and let Andrew's brother John drive me to Northampton. The rest of it you know.''

"Why," he said, shaking his head, "did you never tell me all this?"

"At first I only wanted to forget. As you know better than anyone, it is a hard thing to be driven from your home by scandal and gossip and nasty speculation. And later, when we were at Arcadia, I *did* forget—for a time. I might have told you everything after we were married, but then your cousin came and I learned you were a lord and we quarrelled. If I had known then that you were harbouring such dreadful suspicions about me—but I didn't.'' Gazing steadily at him, she said, "I can understand why you found it easy to believe in my lack of virtue. I am not stupid, and I *do* have a mirror."

Sitting down beside her, Dominic reached for her hand and said huskily, "There is one thing I have to know, Nerissa. If you had it to do again, would you still marry me?"

She lifted her head and gave him a radiant smile, the one he had yearned to see for all the weeks of their marriage. "I regret only that I haven't been the wife you deserved."

When he folded his arms around her, she expelled her breath on a long, blissful sigh, and as the first light of dawn crept into the room, they both tried to forget, for the moment, that their present happiness might be snatched away during the course of this new day.

= 13 =

MANY HOURS LATER, Nerissa opened her eyes and discovered that she was lying in her husband's bed. She sat up, shoving her hair out of her face, and looked down at her blue satin gown, now crushed and creased, possibly beyond repair.

"What's the time?" Dominic enquired sleepily.

The bracket clock on the mantel showed the advanced hour. "Oh my," she gasped, "it's nearly eleven!" But when she felt his fingers idly tracing a path up her bare arm, she decided that it didn't matter.

"Good," he said, pulling her back down to him, "then I have a little while yet to wish my wife a good morning. I think I shall begin just here." He placed his lips on the beauty mark so close to her mouth.

"Nick," Nerissa said when she was able, "we cannot lie abed all day. When are we expected at the magistrates' court?"

"Oh, no," he said, when she wriggled out of his embrace. "You aren't going with me."

"Indeed I will," she informed him.

"I never guessed you would be such a shrew in the morning," he sighed. She made no reply, but went to stand before a looking-glass. He watched as she struggled vainly to repair the wreck of her coiffure. "It might be very awkward for you—Justin says the best we can hope for is a verdict of manslaughter."

She shook her head at him. "I'm not some weak,

helpless creature you must shield from all unpleasantness, surely you know that by now.''

Dominic ran his fingers through his own disordered locks. ''Very well, then. Order some breakfast brought up to your room, enough for two. And coffee. I'll join you as soon as I can. And tell Rose to begin packing for you, because later today, if fortune favours me, we are leaving for Blythe.''

She didn't ask what they would do if he should be committed to trial for murder; it was something she couldn't even consider. And as much as she wanted to believe that all would be well, she was exceedingly nervous about the ordeal that lay ahead. After first making sure that no servants were loitering in the hallway, she returned to her own suite, where she removed her crushed clothes. She performed the ordinary, everyday business of washing and dressing with a sense of urgency, and although it was Rose's habit to linger over the arrangement of her hair, she hurried this delicate operation along as best she could.

When she went to her sitting-room, where James had just laid the breakfast tray on a table drawn up to the giltwood sofa, she found her husband waiting for her. Dominic handed the footman a sealed letter. ''This goes to Elston House,'' he said, ''and you needn't wait for a reply.'' The servant bowed, then hurried off to do his bidding.

Nerissa joined him on the sofa and poured his coffee, presenting it to him with a whimsical smile. ''It is curious, but this morning, for the very first time, I feel as though I am *truly* your wife.''

''Not quite in every way, but I shall remedy that, you may be sure—as soon as we reach Blythe.''

She experienced a surge of delight, which she covered by saying spiritedly, ''You needn't make it sound like a threat.''

''I meant it as a promise,'' he told her, smiling.

Could this be happening, she asked herself. Last night they had reached a promising state of intimacy before she had fallen asleep in his arms, and now he was making love to her over breakfast, on this of all days. It was like being in the middle of a dream and a nightmare all at once. Her senses thoroughly disordered, she looked down at the array of foods before her and said, "I don't think I can eat a thing."

"You will," Dominic replied, in a tone that brooked no argument. "And you'd better, unless you want to swoon in front of the court. While it might well soften the magistrates' hearts towards me, I had rather win my appeal on the evidence."

When it was time to go, she put on a mulberry velvet pelisse and wound a black fur tippet about her throat; to hide her shaking hands, she carried a large muff. If they had been bound for the scaffold, she could not have been more afraid, but she was determined not to show it.

The town carriage, which bore the Blythe crest upon its panel, conveyed them to the police office in Great Marlborough Street, and its arrival was greeted with shouts and exclamations from the waiting public. Nerissa glanced worriedly at Dominic, who said calmly, "You cannot blame them, it isn't every day that a lord comes into this court." And, they soon discovered, not one lord, but many had come. At the front of the crowded chamber they found a host of peers: the Duke of Solway, Viscount Cavender, and the Marquis of Elston. Dominic shook hands with each one and thanked them for coming.

"I have saved two places," Lord Elston announced. "I wasn't sure if her ladyship would come, but I thought it likely." He cast an approving smile upon Nerissa, and she gave him a weak one in return. "Lady Blythe, you shall sit here, between your husband and Lord Cavender."

She took the chair he indicated, and while the gentlemen continued to talk among themselves, she glanced around the room. Seated where she was, she commanded an excellent view. An iron railing separated the spectators from the court, and on the opposite wall was a fireplace, flanked by two doors. The officials of the court were seated behind a wooden desk covered in green baize, and she took careful note of these men who would decide her husband's fate. One was fat and wore a powdered wig that was much too small and a tight, ill-fitting coat, which gave him a comical appearance; the other was old and frail, and his white head trembled with palsy. Neither looked especially fearsome, and both appeared to be considerably bored by the case they were hearing. Dominic's grim-faced barrister, Mr. Peale, was conversing with Justin Blythe, who was there in his capacity as clerk; their black robes lent a decidedly sombre note to the scene.

When the case was called, Mr. Peale rose and approached the bench. There was a continual buzz of voices which prevented Nerissa from hearing what was being said, but at last the noise all around her abated, just as the two magistrates began to review the finding of the initial inquest into the shooting death of Sir Algernon Titus, baronet.

The portly one, whose name was Mr. Blodgett, said, "Mr. Peale, we understand that you have come before us today to argue that Dominic Sebastian Charles Blythe, Baron Blythe, is innocent of the charge of willful murder. Is that correct?"

"It is, sir. Moreover, I can prove that his lordship's purpose in leaving London on fifth October was not to evade the law officers."

Mr. Blodgett glanced at the papers in his hand. "A surgeon who attended at the duel gave the evidence which placed Lord Blythe at the scene. But as that individual had been connected with other vile crimes, Mr. Crane and I chose to disregard his testimony." He nodded at the constable standing on the other side of the room. "You may bring in the first witness."

One of the doors was opened to admit a neatly dressed gentleman of middle years, and Nerissa listened closely as he swore that his testimony was true. She felt certain she had seen him before, but could not recall when or where.

Mr. Blodgett asked the man to state his name and business, to which question he replied, "I am John Frank, proprietor of the Denbigh Arms, an inn at Lutterworth."

"Mr. Frank, do you recognise that gentleman seated just behind the railing, the one in a black coat?"

"I do, your worship," the man answered. "He stopped at my inn one night in October—I believe it was the first week of that month. He came with a lady, and they'd just been wed."

The older magistrate asked in a quavering voice, "How do you know that, Mr. Frank?"

"The gentleman told me so, before he asked to be shown to the best bedchamber." There was a murmur from the crowd, but it subsided when Mr. Frank added, "*And* his lady was wearing a veil over her hat. I'm afraid the young gentleman was rather the worse for drink, and I clearly recall that he said he'd made too many toasts to his bride."

Laughter greeted this statement, and Mr. Blodgett said curtly, "Thank you, that will be all. Mr. Peale, the court has heard that Lord and Lady Blythe spent their wedding night at the Denbigh Arms at Lutterworth. I suppose the gentleman's story can be corroborated?" The barrister inclined his bewigged head and the magistrate said, on a long-suffering note, "Constable, bring in the next witness."

The person who was subsequently led into the court

was a plain-faced young woman clutching a shawl tightly about her hunched shoulders. "State your name and occupation," Mr. Crane told her none too gently.

"Nan Holden, sir."

"And your occupation?" he repeated.

"I'm chambermaid at the Denbigh Arms, sir." When the elderly magistrate asked if she could identify anyone in the court, she glanced fearfully at the immense crowd. After a moment she said, "The lady and the gentleman there."

"Can you tell me where you last saw them?"

"At the inn."

"Did you wait upon either of them?"

The girl considered this. "I took the lady water for washin', and then I helped her to dress, and I arranged her hair. I remember breakin' her scent bottle, too, but she didn't scold me for it."

"Did she address any remarks to you at that time?" The girl stared stupidly at her inquisitor, and her ugly face wore a puzzled frown. "Did she speak to you?" Mr. Crane amended.

"Oh aye," she said, bobbing her head. "She asked me where was her husband, and I said he was bein' shaved."

Nerissa heard the rumble of amusement behind her, but she didn't care. The first two witnesses established a reasonable motive for Dominic's flight from London. She remembered that he had told her she might well save his life a second time, and now she understood: because they had passed themselves off as newlyweds in Lutterworth, he had an alibi. The date of their marriage had never been publicised, and there was no proof anywhere, not even in Gretna, that it had occurred in November, not October.

"Is that the sum of the evidence you mean to present, Mr. Peale?" the portly magistrate asked.

"If it please your worship, there is one more witness, whose evidence will establish beyond doubt that Lord Blythe had no intention of murdering Sir Algernon Titus. I request permission from the bench to undertake the examination myself.''

''Permission is granted, Mr. Peale.'' Mr Blodgett heaved a sigh and gestured to the constable.

Nerissa was conscious of Dominic's sudden intake of breath, and he reached inside her muff to take hold of her hand. She did not know if he intended to provide reassurance, or whether he sought it for himself.

Although the next witness was also a female, she was nothing like poor Nan Holden, being blonde and quite attractive, and fashionably but soberly attired in dove grey silk. When she was sworn to tell the whole truth, Nerissa heard Viscount Cavender, seated on the other side, make an odd, strangled sound low in his throat.

''Madam, will you please state your name,'' the barrister said politely.

''I am Lady Titus.''

Both magistrates eyed her with considerable interest, as did everyone else in the court. Mr. Crane asked if she was the widow of Sir Algernon Titus, baronet, and she nodded, whereupon he instructed Mr. Peale to proceed with the examination.

''Lady Titus, are you acquainted with Baron Blythe?''

The widow glanced at Dominic and it seemed to Nerissa that her tense expression softened. ''Indeed I am, sir, for he was a frequent visitor to our house.''

''How long was Sir Algernon acquainted with his lordship?'' Mr. Peale asked.

Lady Titus shrugged her shoulders. ''For all of Lord Blythe's life, I should think—and that would be upwards of thirty years. His lordship's name was at the top of the list of those persons we invited to our soirée on the fourth of October.''

"And did Lord Blythe attend?" the barrister enquired.

"He did."

Mr. Peale took a turn around the room before continuing with his questioning. "Lady Titus, do you know of any reason why Lord Blythe might have wished to kill your husband?"

"No, none," she said firmly, clearly.

"Can you tell the bench whether Lord Blythe did, in fact, kill your husband when they met at Chalk Farm on the morning of October fifth?"

"He did not."

"And how do you know that?"

"Because my husband was very much alive when Lord Blythe and two other gentlemen brought him home."

Mr. Peale paused to let the magistrates—and the rest of the court—digest this. "And was Sir Algernon conscious? Lucid?"

"Both. I sat with him until the doctor arrived, and he was talking to me all that time."

"Do you remember what he said?"

For the first time during her recital, the witness exhibited signs of distress. Her generous bosom rose and fell, then she said, "He begged me not to be angry with him, and explained that he'd met Dominic Blythe at Chalk Farm, although he did not appear to attach any blame to his lordship for what had happened."

"You are sure of that?"

"Quite sure," she said, "otherwise I would not be standing here now."

Mr. Peale seemed to be unaware that he had just received a setdown, but a ripple of amusement gave evidence of the spectators' appreciation of her ladyship's remark. "Lady Titus," the barrister continued, "when the physician ministered to your husband, did he give an opinion on Sir Algernon's chances of recovery?''

"His opinion meant nothing to me," the lady said harshly. "For it was the doctor killed my husband, and not Lord Blythe.''

This outburst resulted in an intermission, during which the two magistrates conferred with the barrister, and then with one another. At first Nerissa thought the examination was over, but Lady Titus had not yet been dismissed—she still stood before the bench, her chin held high. Her testimony was so precise that it gave the impression of being entirely accurate, and Nerissa was sure it would go a long way towards exonerating Dominic. He must have known that Lady Titus would be present; unlike Lord Cavender, he'd exhibited no surprise when she had stepped into the court. Deep within the warm recesses of her muff, she could feel her husband's hand gripping her own, and she forgot about Ramsey Blythe. "Do you think everything will be all right now?" she whispered.

Dominic smiled down at her. "I am hopeful. Georgiana sounded very convincing, don't you think?"

"Oh yes," she agreed.

When the court officials concluded their brief colloquy, Mr. Blodgett signalled to Mr. Peale to resume the interrogation.

"Lady Titus," he began, "just now you stated that the physician was responsible for Sir Algernon's demise. Would you explain exactly what you meant by that?"

"The doctor insisted that my husband be bled," the lady said wearily. "I protested, but to no avail—medical men dislike having their advice contradicted, especially by a female. If Sir Algernon had been in a high fever, it would have been a different matter entirely, but he was already weak from loss of blood. After being cupped, he grew even weaker. At first I thought he was falling asleep, for the doctor had also given him some laudanum for the pain. And then I was told that he was dead,'' she concluded in a lifeless voice.

''Do you recall where Lord Blythe was during the time you were with your husband?''

''Lord Blythe?'' Georgiana repeated, as though she'd never heard the name before. ''I believe he was downstairs.''

''He did not rush away, or attempt to hide himself from the law?''

''Oh no, he was there. I remember that I went to find him after Sir Algernon—I went to him after it was over. I don't know exactly what I said, but I didn't tell him about—'' Suddenly Georgiana was quiet, and very still.

''About what, Lady Titus?'' Mr. Peale prompted her.

''Forgive me, sir, I'm afraid my mind was wandering,'' she said apologetically. ''Could you repeat your question?''

''What did you say to Lord Blythe?''

''I really can't tell you with any degree of certainty, sir. Very likely I expressed my amazement that Sir Algernon had challenged him. You see, at our party the night before, someone told my husband that Lord Blythe had—had betrayed him. And his lordship was certainly entitled to defend himself against such a base lie.''

Nerissa had the impression that Mr. Peale lost control of the witness, for he seemed to be forming his question as it occurred to him. ''Are you saying that the duel did not result from a quarrel, but was provoked by malicious gossip? Wouldn't Lord Blythe have denied any charge laid against him?''

''I suppose he must have done, only my husband didn't believe him. Sir Algernon was very stubborn—

and of a jealous disposition. I assure you the man who slandered Lord Blythe knew that,'' she said acidly.

''Did your husband have some enemy, was there any person who would have profited from his death?''

Georgiana lifted her golden head. ''An enemy?'' she repeated, a strange smile playing about her lips. ''I can't be sure of that. But my husband and Lord Blythe were equally his victims.''

''Can your ladyship be more specific? Do you know the name of the individual who lied to your husband, thereby inciting his anger?''

''I do. He is in the court.'' On a note of high triumph, she declared, ''The blackguard who was responsible for that duel is Viscount Cavender, Lord Blythe's cousin.''

=== 14 ===

MR. BLODGETT POSSESSED a booming voice, but not
even he had the power to control the din created by
the outraged spectators. Lady Titus, clearly shaken
by the uproar her accusation had created, looked as
though she might fall to the floor. Mr. Peale waited
patiently for order to be restored, and everyone else
was staring at the viscount.

Finally the witness was led away by the constable,
and Nerissa heard Lord Cavender mutter, *"Bitch!"*
through his teeth.

Said Lord Elston curtly, "Be still, Ram, for God's
sake."

"I won't," Ramsey flashed back. "You cool devil,
did you put her up to this? I'll not sit by and let some
whore insult me in public!" He leaned across Nerissa
to speak to Dominic. "Surely *you* don't believe her,
Nick!"

"Which of us did you want out of the way, me or
Sir Algernon?" Dominic asked, his grey eyes hard
and implacable.

"Neither!" Ramsey protested in a fierce whisper.

"Let us say it was both, and damn you for a lying
cur!" Dominic felt his wife grasp his arm as if to
restrain him, but he paid no heed. "Call me out if you
dare—or does the knowledge of your own sins prevent
that? You robbed me of my honour," he said savagely,

"and by so doing you have dishonoured yourself past all reclaim."

His face ashen, Ramsey rose stiffly and hurried out of the court.

After his lordship's abrupt departure, an expectant hush fell over the room as everyone waited to learn what the magistrates would make of this development.

Mr. Blodgett leaned back in his chair. "Mr. Peale, under the present circumstances, I believe we should give our opinion at once."

"I concur," Mr. Crane said faintly. "We need not withdraw, I think, for the matter does not require further deliberation on my part."

His brother magistrate nodded, then said, "In this case, as in all capital cases, the rules of evidence must be strictly observed. At the initial inquest, no one testified that Sir Algernon did not expire upon the duelling ground, and the coroner therefore concluded that the gentleman's opponent not only intended murder, but committed it. After hearing Lady Titus's description of the events of October the fourth and fifth, the bench decrees that the verdict must be overturned." There was an approving hum from the crowd, but Mr. Blodgett quelled it with a glance. "Furthermore, this examination has revealed that after the obligatory exchange of fire, Baron Blythe demonstrated his concern for the baronet's welfare. He conveyed his wounded friend to London, at some risk to himself—hardly the act of a ruthless murderer. As to the lady's charge that a physician is responsible for her husband's demise, this court has no authority to have the accused bound over for prosecution. It's not the first time a man has been doctored into a premature grave, nor will it be the last. Our finding is accidental death. This case is dismissed."

Dominic turned to Nerissa and murmured, " 'O wise and upright judge.' "

"It's *over,*" she breathed, although she couldn't quite accept the truth of it. He assisted her to her feet, and they found their exit impeded by the many well-wishers who crowded in upon them.

The Duke of Solway said, "I'm vastly relieved—this is the outcome your friends hoped for. Still, Blythe, you would do well to remove from town as soon as possible."

"That is my intention, Your Grace."

"Good, good. There's nothing you can—or should—do for Cavender. If he is cut by the whole of his acquaintance tomorrow, it is no more than he deserves. Well, I must be on my way—the duchess will be anxious to learn what has transpired. My dear," he said, smiling at Nerissa, "we hope to have the pleasure of seeing you and your husband at the Haberdine Castle very soon."

As the duke departed, Justin Blythe stepped forward to claim Dominic's attention. His bony face was a mask of strain, but his voice was steady as he said, "My hasty trip to Lutterworth was quite unnecessary, it seems—for Lady Titus won the case for us. But at such a cost—" Turning on Lord Elston, standing behind him, he said, "Damon, you are the one who persuaded her ladyship to give her evidence. Did you know she would implicate my brother?"

"I warned her that no good would come of introducing Ram's name, but evidently Georgiana is ruled by a very strict sense of justice."

Justin's brown eyes were sombre. "I must find Ram—he will need me."

As the young clerk made his solitary way out of the court, Lord Elston observed, "I suspect Justin's ambition to become a barrister has received a grave setback this day. What can we do for him, I wonder? Have someone pull a string or two at the Foreign Office?"

"The diplomatic service? Yes, a posting abroad might be just the thing for him, especially now," Dominic said thoughtfully, his eyes still following the black-gowned figure.

Nerissa, who had kept silent all this time, spoke up. "I can't believe Mr. Blythe would agree to leave the country—he won't want to desert his brother at such a time."

Lord Elston said grimly, "That is why it will fall to Ramsey to persuade him to take whatever position we find for him. Well, Nick, shall we be off? I had your note this morning, and I must say I went to some considerable trouble to arrange everything as you requested."

"What is he talking about?" Nerissa asked, glancing from her husband to the marquis, and back.

"Come with us, and you shall see," Dominic invited her.

Their short walk took them to the stately, columned edifice of the church which dominated George Street. There was a post-chaise standing at the curb, an array of luggage strapped behind. Nerissa demanded to know why it was waiting for them there, but neither of her escorts would give her a direct answer.

They halted beneath the portico of St. George's, and her husband said to his friend, "Will you kindly stop ogling my wife and inform the vicar that we will be with him presently?" When the marquis had withdrawn, Dominic took Nerissa's hand. "Today my life and my honour have been restored to me—I am a free man, Nerissa. We began so badly, you and I, and although that ridiculous ceremony at Gretna may be legal and binding, it was frightfully ill-managed. I had Damon procure a special licence for us—it occurred to me that you might wish to have our union blessed by church rite."

"But I don't."

Perplexed by her unequivocal reply, he asked, "Whyever not?"

Her blue eyes bright with mischief, Nerissa said, "Because a marriage which cannot be proved can *never* be dissolved."

"You can't seriously think I would ever take such a step!"

"Oh, I do hope not," she said fervently. "But I rather like the security of knowing that it would be quite out of your power." She lifted her smiling face to his and reminded him, "I already gave you my vow to abide with you, for better or for worse, at Gretna. And, Nick, the worst must surely be behind us now."

When Lord Elston returned, he enquired, with exaggerated politeness, if they were coming inside, and Dominic, beaming at his wife, replied, "We have made up our minds to dispense with the services of the vicar after all."

"Afraid I would demand the privilege of kissing the bride?" was his friend's mocking rejoinder.

"Something of the kind," Dominic laughed. "Will you give the reverend gentleman my compliments, and my apologies, and—"

"A handsome fee," the marquis sighed.

After discharging his duties, he followed Lord Blythe and his lady to the chaise. "I'm sure you're impatient to be gone, but I really *must* have that kiss," he said slyly, and before Dominic could say him nay, he embraced Lady Blythe and bussed her soundly on the cheek. "Have a safe journey, my dear, and if your husband should turn out to be a brute, you have only to let me know and I'll come to rescue you!"

"I have no such fear, my lord," she assured him.

"As for you, Nick," Lord Elston continued, "you mustn't worry about Justin, for I will see to it that he doesn't suffer his brother's disgrace."

As the chaise moved forward, Dominic leaned back

against the seat and said, "I think you will like Blythe, Nerissa. For a very long time now I've wanted to take you there, but my case seemed so desperate I thought this day would never come." He paused to put his thoughts in order, for her joyous smile threatened to wipe from his mind the many important and necessary things he wanted to tell her. "You saved my life, not once but many times—and my sanity, because you gave me hope when I'd lost everything else. And when I nearly lost *you,* I realised that nothing else mattered very much, not even the possibility that you had a child. Last night I discovered, to my horror, that I have wronged you, and for that I am more sorry than I have ever been in my life. I married you, believing you were something you are not, and loved you despite that." He caught the past tense and amended hastily, "And will always love you, although I don't really know you as I thought I did."

"But you *do* know me," Nerissa hastened to say, "for I haven't changed. I'm still as impulsive and stubborn and wild and willful as I ever was. But there is something you have yet to learn about me," she realised suddenly. "In all my twenty-three years I've been fond of very few people. Papa and my aunt are gone now. Andrew was a good friend, but could never be anything more to me. For a time I had Samuel, but he isn't really mine to love. My heart would be quite empty, Nick, if I hadn't met you. I first knew my own feelings at Arcadia, when I found Cat's letter. And then, when I saw my godson yesterday, I thought that perhaps by giving you a child I might be able to win your love."

"You stand in no need of help, Nerissa," he assured her. "Any child of ours would be proof of my love." He took her face in his hands and said huskily, "From this time and forever, you must be happy. If you aren't, it won't be through any fault of mine, for I intend to do everything in my power to make you so.''

And he began by kissing her long and longingly as they left the great city behind and followed the road to a new and brighter future together.